Praise for Ladett

"Quietly moving."—*New York Times Book Review*

"Stark and engrossing, this debut novel . . . fixes an empathetic but relentless gaze on a woman determined to expunge the regrets from her life. . . . An immersing achievement, this novel should please any fan of good fiction."—*Publishers Weekly*

"A poignantly written, lovely novel of the heartland that honors the best traditions of storytelling."—JIM HARRISON, author of *The English Major* and *Legends of the Fall*

"This is good, old-fashioned storytelling at its best, and Mary Rasmussen will live forever in your hearts as a young woman who faces enormous tests and survives in order to protect those she loves."—JONIS AGEE, author of *The River Wife*

"Randolph's characters peel back the stereotypes, all the while exploring the truths and half-truths of the iconic Sandhills family, feisty, fecund, and invincible."—*Western American Literature*

"Randolph has worked hard to get the Sandhills language right; she clearly has enormous respect for the ranching culture."
—*Los Angeles Times*

"A nearly perfect book. The harsh Nebraska landscape is a complete character in its own right. Unforgiving. Somewhat distant. Aloof. Home. The human characters are more yielding, but only just. And the sum of what author Ladette Randolph creates here is unforgettable."—*January Magazine*

FLYOVER FICTION SERIES | *Series editor:* Ron Hansen

Haven's
Wake

Ladette Randolph

University of Nebraska Press | Lincoln & London

Publication of this volume was assisted by a grant from the
Friends of the University of Nebraska Press.

Library of Congress Cataloging-in-Publication Data
Randolph, Ladette.
Haven's wake / Ladette Randolph.
p. cm.— (Flyover fiction)
ISBN 978-0-8032-4357-6 (pbk.: alk. paper) 1. Mennonites—
Nebraska—Fiction. 2. Family secrets—Fiction. 3. Domestic
fiction. I. Title.
PS3618.A644H38 2013
813'.6—dc23   2012033405

Set in Granjon by Laura Wellington
Designed by Roger Buchholz

For Noel, with love

And I sought for a man among them, that should make up the hedge, and stand in the gap before me for the land, that I should not destroy it: but I found none.

Ezekiel 22:30

Acknowledgments

A special thanks to the first readers of this manuscript: Bronwyn and Jordan Milliken and Tami and Briana Turnbull. Their sound advice set me on my way. Many thanks to my agent, Janet Silver, who steered my course, and thanks as well to Chris Castellani, Bret Anthony Johnston, and Heidi Pitlor for being excellent readers all and providing support and encouragement at a crucial time in the journey. I owe too much to my colleague and friend Pamela Painter to acknowledge it fairly. She kept me steady on my path more than once when I thought I couldn't continue. To Sherrie Flick and Bill Lychack — both writers whom I admire and who gave me invaluable advice on the final draft — I offer my sincerest gratitude. Thank you especially to Kristen Elias Rowley, my editor at the University of Nebraska Press, and the publishing professionals at UNP who made a safe harbor for this book. I'm deeply grateful to Elizabeth Gratch for her keen eye in copyediting. And as always, thanks to my husband, Noel, my first and best reader, the one who sees most clearly the map and beyond.

Haven's
Wake

JULY 10, 2009

At 3:00 a.m. Elsa Grebel made her way downstairs through the dark house to her piano. She wore only her white nightgown, forgetting even now the house was full of guests. Her hair, un-pinned for the night, hung to her waist and warmed her bare arms. A breeze rustled the curtains at the window next to the piano. Outside she heard a screech owl whinny. Around her, in the shadows of the room, were the familiar artifacts of her long life in this house with her husband, Haven.

She started out softly, reluctant to compete with the night sounds, knowing from memory the hymns she played. "The Un-clouded Day," "On Christ the Solid Rock I Stand," "The Church's One Foundation," "Abide with Me," "Blessed Assurance":

> Blessed assurance, Jesus is mine!
> Oh what a foretaste of glory divine.
> Heir of salvation, purchase of God,
> born of His spirit, washed in His blood.
>
> *This is my story, this is my song,*
> *praising . . .*

Sensing a presence in the room, she stopped and looked behind her. In the darkness Elsa saw a man sitting in the overstuffed chair where Haven sat every evening.

"Haven."

"No, Mother. It's Jonathan. Sing with me."

She paused and turned back to the piano but kept her hands in her lap for a few moments, unsure if she could go on. Finally, she continued, her alto joining Jonathan's baritone, the piano carrying the melody. They sang like this every verse of every song, Jonathan remembering the words, surprising her after so many years away. A lost soul, and still he could sing like this. Only God's grace would help her forgive him his latest trespass. He'd broken her heart years ago, and he'd broken it again the night before. She supposed, though, a mother could never completely give up on her own child.

By four thirty Elsa's three sisters and their husbands had joined them, bringing out their lap harps and guitars. At five the sun had started to rise. One of the barn cats leapt onto the window screen next to the piano, and Elsa's rooster greeted the day. They were singing in four-part harmony at full volume, a regular congregation, making no effort to quiet themselves, when Timothy stumbled downstairs, hair standing on end, Anna June following close behind him. They'd both been sleeping in Elsa's room.

"What's going on?" Timothy said, stopping short of the bottom stair and surveying with contempt the gathering of his elders in their nightclothes. He didn't disguise his disgust both at being awakened in this way and at having to confront the vagaries of those half-clothed, aging bodies. That stopped them all for a few seconds, the look on Timothy's face, and they laughed midway through "Count Your Many Blessings" before Elsa regained her composure and picked up again where she'd left off, everyone joining in to end the sing along on a resounding and triumphal note. "Count your blessings, name them one by one.

4

Count your many blessings, see what God hath done."

Timothy, his question left unanswered, still stood perplexed in the stairwell. Any hope there may have been that he would join in the chorus ended when he abruptly went into the kitchen to start a pot of coffee. The rooster again, and that, coupled with Timothy's inept slamming of cupboard doors and rattling around the kitchen — where counters were laden with gifts of food from well-wishers across Seward County — finally rallied everyone. Each singer retreated into his or her self. Elsa felt exposed without her robe and reached for an afghan lying on a nearby chair. The murky light of dawn brought the room out of shadow where before them lay a day of hard work. It started with the funeral.

For three days Elsa had been resisting her sisters' bossy ways. Now, at first light it started again, Eleanor reminding her as she put away her lap harp, "Elsa May, you need to be making some decisions about the memorial fund."

Emily and Evelyn said nothing, but Elsa intercepted the glance they exchanged when she didn't respond to Eleanor's comment. They weren't the brightest of women, her sisters. Elsa had long ago realized this, and their habit of still treating her like a silly kid, their baby sister, only confirmed it. They wore their robes loosely sashed, and Elsa couldn't help but make other comparisons: the purple-veined legs, the calloused heels and twisted, tortured toes. They were elderly women after all. What startled Elsa this morning was seeing it all so exposed before they had donned their customary prayer veils and cotton dresses, their hose and Sass shoes. But more than that, they were all fat. And why wouldn't they be? All they did was think about food — barely finishing one meal before starting to plan for the next. She hadn't counted to ten before Emily said, "I'd better be getting dressed. Everyone will be wanting breakfast."

Elsa felt the tiniest bit of remorse for being critical of her sisters, but what other defense did she have against their relentless ganging up on her? It had been like this when they were growing up together. The three of them — teenagers when she was still a little girl — had felt free to criticize her, the youngest of eight. Her brothers had never gotten involved with trying to mold her, as her sisters had. No wonder Marian had been so exasperated with them after she married their father. They'd always thought they knew what was best for Elsa. No use fighting now. They'd all be leaving soon.

JULY 6, 2009

There had been rain in the night, but this morning the sun was out, that dripping, golden light Jonathan Grebel loved so much about New England summers. There hadn't been sunshine for weeks, rain every day through June, tempting Jonathan this morning to stay home from work.

Nina, off for the summer, was already out working in her gardens. The rambling Victorian they'd restored at the peak of Chestnut had a sprawling lawn that sloped down to the curb, a rarity in Jamaica Plain, and Nina kept perennial gardens everywhere.

Over their years together Nina had filled the house with strays she'd adopted of all kinds, both people and animals. Right now they had only animals living with them. Their turtle, Glen, had free rein in the house but favored a spot by the refrigerator. As Jonathan held the door open this morning in his search for the butter, Glen slowly climbed up on his back legs and stretched his neck upward, hoping for a crumb of something. Jonathan gave him a small leaf of lettuce before closing the refrigerator door. He called for Lolita, their black pug, and she came running into the kitchen with a clatter. In addition to Glen and Lolita were two cats, Todd and Henry, and a canary Jonathan had dubbed Bait because of the way the cats had eyed the poor fellow when Nina brought him home.

Before leaving for work, Jonathan shouted good-bye to Nina from the back door. She waved a gloved hand in his direction. "Don't let the cats out," she called, and only then did he notice between his feet the yellow kitten.

"Nina!"

"Isn't he adorable? I found him at the Stony Brook stop last night. He was soaked from the rain."

Jonathan caught the kitten as it made for the open door. "Nina," he said again, but she'd turned back to her work and conveniently ignored him. "Farmer in the fucking dell," he grumbled as he closed the door and set the kitten on the floor.

Later he got off the T at Mass Ave. so he could enjoy the sun and walk through the Southwest Corridor and Copley Square to his office across from the Public Garden. He and his partner, Monty Pipher, had rented the space thirteen years ago in spite of its poor condition because of the windows overlooking the garden. The business was still small, only he and Monty and their assistant, Jennifer. Each year they held a competition for a summer intern. Sara, their intern this summer, was a grad student from RISD. She was creative and probably brilliant, but she was such a pain in the ass around the office, Jonathan had wanted to let her go since she'd started in May. Monty, who hated confrontation, had so far persuaded Jonathan to ride out the summer with her.

As Jonathan came off the elevator this morning, he heard Sara on Jennifer's phone. He listened long enough to figure out she was talking to Murray Schiffman, one of their major clients, a contractor who only accepted projects over two million dollars. Sara was arguing with him, using that tone of voice Jonathan couldn't stand, condescending as hell and hard to take.

To top it off, she kept calling Murray by his first name. It irked Jonathan, though he didn't know what she should call Murray instead. Well, the truth was, she shouldn't be talking to him at all.

He noticed Jennifer making copies in the other room and had the distinct impression she was somehow doing Sara's bidding. Unbelievably, when he gestured for Sara to transfer the call to him, she frowned and shook her head. Monty came in while she was still on the phone, and Jonathan met him in his office before he could even drop his bag.

"She's got to go, Monty."

"Jesus. Good morning to you too."

"I mean it, Monty. I'm sacking her today. She's out there arguing with Murray, talking to him like he's a preschooler. I've been patient enough —"

"Patient? You? Jonathan, you're a lot of things, but —"

"She's a disaster."

"She's done amazing work for us already this summer." Monty set his bag on the floor beside his desk. "You just don't like her. Be honest about it."

"You act like that doesn't matter. She's bad for business."

Monty didn't respond. Instead, he sat down behind his desk and held out his coffee cup toward Jonathan.

Jonathan took the cup. "This your way of changing the subject?"

"This is my way of saying let's talk to her after she finishes her call, but I'm going to need more caffeine before that happens." He paused and smiled. "I assume this is going to be a teachable moment?"

"Fuck you, Monty."

Monty laughed. Nina had one time used the phrase teachable moment in a conversation with Monty, and he'd never let

Jonathan live it down. Nina had worked in some of the toughest school districts in the city before being hired by the state board of education as a teacher trainer. She was an optimist. Where Jonathan saw hopeless, Nina saw potential. Monty, who'd known Jonathan for over thirty years, could never quite get over the fact that they'd made the marriage work for as long as they had, almost twenty years now.

On his way back to Monty's office Jonathan noticed Sara was off the phone, and he gestured for her to follow him. Before she sat down, the phone rang again. "I need to get that," she said.

"Let the machine pick it up," Jonathan said.

"But Jennifer asked me to watch the phone."

This was what got to him. Where did you start with someone like this? "Sara," Jonathan said. "You're a talented designer. I don't have any doubt you'll have a grand career, but you have a lot to learn."

By the time he got back to his desk an hour later, Sara was still crying in Monty's office. Jonathan wasn't convinced her tears were sincere, and quite frankly he didn't care. Still, he hadn't intended to cause such a kerfuffle first thing in the morning. As he listened to his phone messages, he wondered if maybe they should reconsider the whole internship thing next year.

The first message was from Murray. It had come in last night. "I'm over here on Marlborough. Where are the goddamned lights? I don't have the schematics. I don't have shit from your office." So that was what Sara had been dealing with this morning. Jonathan knew for a fact everything had been delivered to the work site. He'd walked the schematics over himself late yesterday afternoon, and the lights had been there when he'd arrived. He'd talked to Murray's project manager. As usual, Murray'd gone off half-cocked. Maybe Sara had it right. Maybe Murray was a preschooler.

The last message he listened to was a garbled affair from his mother. She hated the phone and never called him. She'd obviously been nervous about the answering machine, starting the message before the tape came on, so he heard only, "Your father's dead. You'll probably want to come home."

Anna June Grebel loved to spend the night at her friend Celia's house. Celia's bedroom was pink, and she had a canopy bed, but the best thing was how you could climb out one of the windows in her room and sit on the roof. They did it late at night so they could look at the stars. They always took Celia's dog, Fritz, with them. He was a black and brown dachshund. Celia called him a wiener dog. Anna June wanted a dog, but her mom always said no. She said Anna June wouldn't take care of it, which was a total lie. Anna June had begged and begged. She'd promised she'd feed it every day and clean up after it. She'd asked for a dog every birthday and every Christmas, until finally Daddy had said, "Enough of that. I'm putting my foot down. No dogs. Not ever."

After that Celia said Fritz could be Anna June's dog too. Whenever Anna June spent the night, Celia let Fritz sleep with her, and she let Anna June hold him on the roof. He was a good dog. It was partly because of Fritz that Anna June always spent the night at Celia's house and Celia never spent the night at her house. But it was other things too. People didn't always understand about Daddy.

She and Celia had stayed out on the roof a long time the night before talking about everything. Anna June was going to be a farmer when she grew up, but right now she was working with Grandpa so she could learn. Celia liked to tell stories about girls who lived in outer space on different stars and how the star girls could see them. Anna June liked those stories. She was good at drawing, and they both drew pictures of the star girls.

"They have very good eyesight," Celia said. "They can see us. They have transmitters," Celia said as she drew. "We need transmitters so we can talk to them." They both thought for a long time about where to get transmitters. Fritz had felt hot where he was curled up on Anna June's lap. Her legs got sweaty, and the roof shingles scratched. When she moved, Fritz jumped up.

"Be careful," Celia said. "He's likely to jump off the roof."

"He wouldn't do that."

"Don't put it past him."

They were going into the fifth grade. Celia was already eleven. Anna June wouldn't turn eleven until November. One of the girls in their church had gotten her period already. She wore a bra. They talked about that too. Mostly, though, they talked about the True Secret History. Anna June always had a new story. She told Celia a story that night about a family that had moved away a long time ago.

"They lived in Bethel and went to church for about a month," Anna June said while she drew a picture of one of the star girls. "They had about ten kids, and they lived in a house on the Blue River. One night the father killed the mother. He said it was an accident with the gun." This was the best sad story Anna June had ever heard.

"That's terrible," Celia said.

"It gets worse than that. He told everybody it was an accident, that the gun went off accidentally. At first everybody believed him. They felt terrible for him. But then the lady's sister, who'd been staying there, told the police he'd done it on purpose. She told them he was a mean man and he was mean to his wife and kids. The kids all had to go live with different relatives after that. He went to jail, and it was a terrible time for the church."

"Your dad told you that?"

"Yep. Grandma only told me the family had some trouble and went to Bethel church a little while, but Daddy told me the real story." Anna June's dad knew a lot of things, and when he was in a mood, he'd talk to her. Anna June didn't tell Celia the stories the way her dad told them. He said bad words sometimes. Her mom told her never to repeat those words.

The best thing about her dad was when he played his guitar and sang. He wrote good songs, and her mom always said he had a beautiful voice. Anna June thought he could be on the radio he was so good, and when Celia heard the CD, Celia thought so too. He was teaching Anna June how to play the guitar. The strings hurt her fingers something terrible. Sometimes her dad got fed up with her and said she was too stupid to learn, but other times he told her with some practice she could be a good guitar player.

Celia's mom made waffles in the morning. She always made Anna June's favorite things when she stayed over.

"Anna June," Celia's mother said. "If it doesn't rain this afternoon, I'm going to take Celia to the pool in Seward. Would you like to go along?"

"I'll have to see what Grandpa's doing first."

"If he doesn't have any work for you, you'd be welcome to come with us."

Celia's mother was pretty and young, and Celia's dad had built their house. It was the nicest house in Bethel. If it hadn't been for Grandpa, Anna June would have wanted to live with

Celia. Anna June's mom and dad were old. Her two older sisters, Susan and Laurie, were the same age as Celia's mom and dad.

Anna June wasn't even finished with her waffles that morning when her mom came for her, surprising them when she knocked on the front door. Anna June didn't think she'd ever eat waffles again in her life.

That year the corn in eastern Nebraska stood ten feet tall by early July, and rain fell steadily across the state through the spring and now into summer, replenishing the groundwater and bringing to an end nearly a decade of drought. Old-timers claimed they'd never seen such a year for crops. It seemed too good to be true. Everyone that summer watched the sky for trouble: flash floods, tornadoes, straight winds, or hail, all the ways there were to destroy in minutes their hopes for the year. Instead, every day, afternoon rains passed through quickly without damage, leaving in their wake a radiant sun in another cloudless sky.

In Seward County, among field after field of soybeans and corn, were small patchwork fields of organic oats, barley, and popcorn belonging to Haven and Elsa Grebel. It was early morning, and Elsa was finishing her outside chores. She didn't bother with the men's work in the field; rather, each summer day she tended to her vegetable and flower gardens and to her chickens. As a girl, she'd tried every way she could think of to move the hens off their eggs without creating a frenzy, but she'd long ago learned that no hen would give up her eggs without a fight. This morning the outraged chickens were pacing and grumbling as

Elsa left the coop with a bucket full of eggs, her old Rhode Island Red rooster keeping his distance against the fence.

She would clean the eggs and sell them in Lincoln at the Open Harvest food co-op, where they would give her $2.50 a dozen and in turn ask their customers to pay $3.50 for that same dozen, all because of the way she treated her chickens, as if allowing them to roam free and giving them decent grain to eat was exceptional.

"I haven't forgotten about you, Red," Elsa said, opening the gate. "You'll get your treat later."

By midmorning she'd completed her household chores and finished writing the church newsletter. There'd been a lot to report about recent Mennonite relief actions around the world. Their efforts had been stretched thin in the spring and summer of 2009 as war displaced so many. Wars and rumors of wars. Their congregation had sent a disaster relief team to Italy a month earlier to help with the earthquake victims there. Two more teams would leave soon for Pakistan to help with the refugees from the Swat Valley. The work before them never ended. Elsa had just brought out her file cards for the community history — she found if she did a little every day it added up — when she saw Alvin Schweitzer's truck pull into the yard. She met him at the kitchen door as he walked up to the house. He looked so hangdog, his cap in his hand, she had to laugh as she pushed open the screen, "Alvin, did you run over another one of my chickens?"

Alvin dropped his head before looking up again. "I sure wish that was it, Elsa. I sure do." He could barely keep his eyes on her. "Elsa, it's Haven."

She felt her heart start to kick hard. "What are you saying, Alvin?"

Alvin shook his head and looked at her with a beseeching expression. "Oh, Elsa. He's gone. Haven's gone."

"Don't," Elsa said. "Don't." She backed into the kitchen, letting the screen door slam shut between them, leaving Alvin on the porch alone.

"Elsa."

"Don't you come here telling me —"

"He didn't suffer none, Elsa," Alvin said and went on to tell her about the accident, though she could barely hear a word he was saying.

Alvin opened the screen door and stepped into the kitchen, but Elsa slapped at his hands as he tried to catch her in a hug. "Don't —"

"I'm sure sorry, Elsa. Doreen'll be over soon. I'll wait here with you until she comes."

"No, I don't want you here, Alvin."

"Well, that's fine, Elsa. I'll just wait outside in case you need anything."

"No, I don't want you here. Go on home."

"I can't do that, Elsa. I can't leave you alone like that."

"Suit yourself," Elsa said and closed the screen door. She paused before closing and locking the storm door too. She didn't want anyone fussing around her. She glanced back out the window at Alvin standing alone on the porch and noticed how his shoulders slumped. He was an old man, and he'd just found his friend dead by the pond, an accident with the tractor; that's all she knew. Alvin didn't have any more for her than that. "He didn't suffer none," Alvin had repeated before she'd closed the door, and she clung to that bit of mercy now. He hadn't suffered. She looked again and saw Alvin put his cap back on. She didn't much like him waiting there like that, like he was a sentry guarding her, but she saw he wasn't going to leave.

When Elsa returned to her kitchen, which only minutes before had been her refuge on a sweet summer morning, she found instead a place she didn't recognize. In the quiet she heard her chickens clucking and scratching in the yard. Above the sink the old rooster clock — a gift for their thirty-fifth anniversary — ticked loudly in the silent house. She felt herself begin to shake, and a rasping sob burst from her throat. And only then did she think to pray.

The linoleum was hard beneath her knees. "Lord," she said. And she called out again, "Lord?" Only silence. She felt as if the floor had opened up beneath her and she was spinning in the universe alone. Not falling through space but suspended in darkness, moving farther and farther away while watching herself and her house grow smaller, minute, minuscule, a speck, then nothing.

Elsa was stiff and her knees swollen by the time she finally stood up, restored to her proper self, wrapped once more in the warmth of the Lord's love and solace. Outside Alvin still waited patiently. She opened the door. "I'm sorry for how I behaved earlier, Alvin. I'm sorry. Come on in. You should wait inside. Let me get you a cup of coffee."

"No need, Elsa. I don't want to add to your troubles."

Elsa didn't say anything as she opened the screen door wider and waited for Alvin to come inside. She poured him a cup of coffee and set it on the kitchen counter. Her hand shook so she was afraid she'd spill it if she handed it to him.

"Is there someone you'd like me to notify, Elsa?" Alvin said.

"I'll let the boys know myself. Could you please give me a bit of privacy and take your coffee into the living room?" Alvin nodded and reluctantly left the kitchen with his coffee cup. Elsa could see she was making him uncomfortable, but she couldn't do any more for him right now.

The radio on the counter buzzed with static as she summoned Jeffrey's house down the road. Her daughter-in-law, Kathy, picked up, and before she could finish her greeting, Elsa said, "You've got to tell Jeffrey, Kathy."

"What's that, Mother Grebel?"

"Gently, Kathy. You've got to let Jeffrey know his daddy's dead."

"Oh, it can't be. What happened?"

"All's I know is it was an accident with the tractor. They say he didn't suffer. Let Jeffrey know that. He didn't suffer."

Kathy paused a long time. Elsa thought she might be crying. "I don't know how I'm going to tell Anna June," Kathy said finally. "We'll be right over."

"Don't push Jeffrey now," Elsa said before she hung up. She knew Kathy could push him sometimes. He was fragile, and she could push him.

Elsa hesitated a few minutes before finally picking up the phone to call Jonathan. He'd given them trouble over the years, and she was still rehearsing what she would tell him when that fancy machine of his came on. Everything she'd planned to say rushed out before she heard, "You've reached the desk of Jonathan Grebel, president of Light Works."

JULY 7, 2009

Anna June had gone to Grandpa's pickup first thing after she'd heard about what happened. She could smell him there: grease from his shop, his shaving lotion, his sweaty cap. His work gloves were on the truck seat, and she took them home with her. She didn't ask Grandma. She put them in her drawer along with her box of secret cards.

When Anna June had felt bad in the middle of the night, she'd taken Grandpa's gloves out of the drawer and sniffed them. Whenever she did that, she could hear what Grandpa would say to her. He'd say, "Now, A.J., you be a good girl. Your grandma needs you." He was always saying Grandma needed everyone. He'd say, "Your dad isn't strong. Your mom's working hard. You'll need to listen for what the Lord wants you to do."

You know, God didn't talk to Anna June at all. She listened, but she didn't hear a thing. She heard other things. She heard the ocean underground in Nebraska. If she laid her ear down to the ground, she could hear it. Grandpa said that wasn't possible, but she heard it anyway. She heard things people didn't say out loud. She heard memories in the grass of the pasture. They were the memories of people she didn't know from the olden days. She saw things, too, like the hedge of angels finished, standing guard over the aquifer — that was what the underground ocean was called. Grandpa had said people were poisoning the water in the aquifer. Their farm was a good farm, but she worried about the water.

She knew the water in the pond wasn't the aquifer, but the hedge of angels was her vision. Grandpa had shared the vision with her. He always said he loved the people of the world. He talked about the poor people without water for their crops and how that was the reason he'd invented his pump a long time ago. He said, "I know it isn't right, A.J., but sometimes I'm proud of that old pump. It's raised a lot of crops and a lot of kids in the world." He'd invented the pump before she was born, before even her dad was born, and Grandpa had told her a girl her size, no "bigger than a grasshopper," could peddle it and bring water to her family's crops. He'd told her there were a lot of little villages around the world where they still used his pump.

She'd been proud of him too. He'd invented other things, but the pump was the best. It was even called "Haven's Pump." She didn't know what she was going to do without Grandpa. He was her favorite person in the world. They'd gone around together. He'd taken her on chores with him. When he was doing something on the farm, he said all the time, "What would you do, A.J.?" She would think hard about whatever he asked about because he always asked real questions. Most grown-ups didn't ask a person real questions.

Mr. Slocum had stopped by to say hello to her this morning. She and Celia had been sitting under the elm tree next to the barn after she'd brought Grandpa's gloves back to the truck. It hadn't been right, her taking them. "I was looking for you up to the house," he said to her.

"I don't like to be there."

"Can't say that I blame you. This is a darned old day, isn't it, little lady?"

Mr. Slocum wasn't Mennonite, but he was good English. He talked to her like she was a person. He was the only other farmer like Grandpa in the county. He'd stop by sometimes, or Grandpa would go over to his place on the Blue River. Anna June liked going there. He had horses and goats and rabbits. He made Grandpa laugh. He'd always say, "Why be difficult, when with a little effort you can be impossible," and every time he said it, Grandpa laughed like he'd never heard it before. Mr. Slocum told stories about silly things people did, like running their trucks under overpasses that were too low or driving away from gas pumps with the hose still in their trucks. He said one time about a neighbor's farmhouse, "They cut so many corners, it's almost a roundhouse." He'd say sometimes, if something was scary, "Now that'll put religion in you." Anna June never understood what he meant by that, and Grandpa never explained.

Mr. Slocum traveled around and went to meetings for organic farmers. He'd told Grandpa last time they'd been over there about a lady he'd met in Missouri named Throckmorten — Jodie Throckmorten — who had milk cows and made organic cheese. "She reads books to those damned cows, don't you know," Mr. Slocum said. "Books by Jane Austen and things like Huck Finn, Wuthering Heights, Madame Bovary, Moby-Dick, things like that. Craziest, goddamnedest thing you ever heard." Grandpa didn't seem to notice when Mr. Slocum said damned or goddamned, which he did a lot. "She names those cheeses she makes," Mr. Slocum said, "after the book she's been reading to the cow it supposedly came from. That's her marketing trick, don't you see? Elizabeth Bennet Camembert; Huck's Hard Cheddar; Mo-Brie Dick."

Grandpa had laughed and laughed when he heard that. "Don't

that beat all," Grandpa had said. "That's what people like, you say?"

"That's it. They eat that up. She was selling cheese like a gangster at the market she worked."

After they had left, Grandpa said to Anna June. "You're all ears, aren't you, A.J."? She didn't say anything, and Grandpa didn't try to make up for Mr. Slocum being the way he was.

Mr. Slocum said now, "You come on over to my place anytime you'd like, you hear me, little lady." Anna June nodded. "I'll sure miss seeing you," he said, "and your grandpa."

Anna June thought it was nice he said that, but she knew she'd never go. How would she ever get over there without Grandpa? She felt even sadder thinking about that. Everything she thought about anymore made her sadder because everything was wrong now.

As soon as Jonathan and Nina had pulled into the driveway of the farm the evening before, Jonathan experienced a familiar heaviness of spirit, a weight that felt like a particular kind of bad weather. It had been two years since he'd been home, ten years since he'd last seen the place in summer. It was greener than usual for July, a result of the rains his father had been telling him about when he called Jonathan each week. Otherwise, little had changed since he'd left home forty years earlier, at the age of eighteen. The outbuildings had been recently painted, the weeds newly shredded around the farmyard, and the farm implements were all in their place. His father always kept things neat.

"You all right?" Nina asked.

He nodded. "You sure you're up for this, Nina?"

"I want to be here with you." Nina looked out the passenger side window toward the house. "It's been a long time." She hadn't been back with him for over six years.

As usual, with any return to the farm Jonathan wanted to go to the barn first rather than to the house, but he went to the house first anyway. Inside he found his mother's orderly kitchen transformed, chaotic with visitors, every available space cluttered with offerings of food he knew had been brought by neighbors and church members. He didn't see his mother, but his aunts all took turns giving him bosomy hugs, grappling a little in the process, so that he felt like they were fighting over him. He didn't mind the feeling.

"Oh, Jonathan, it's you." And there was his mother. Thin, immaculate, her steel gray hair gathered, like her sisters', under a prayer veil. He felt her thinness as he hugged her. All bones, like hugging a bundle of broomsticks.

"They say he didn't suffer," she said. "That's merciful, isn't it?"

Jonathan looked quickly toward his aunts, who all discreetly looked away. When it came to his mother, he was on his own. She would have ignored Nina, except Nina stepped in and embraced her in one of her lingering hugs. His mother may have struggled, but it wouldn't have mattered. Nina was a big woman and a strong one. She held on tight. After Nina released her, his mother staggered slightly. She looked embarrassed as she brushed down her dress and the apron she wore over it when she was at home.

"I've put the two of you in the downstairs bedroom," she said. "It'll be cooler for you there." Jonathan took this as a pointed remark, given his parents refusal a few years ago of his offer to install central air, his father saying, "That's good of you, Son, but give that money instead to someone who really needs it." Jonathan could never do anything for them without it turning into a kind of contest.

Elsa started to lead them to their room, but Jonathan stopped her. "Mother, don't worry about us. We know the way."

"Of course," she said, and he heard the hurt in her voice. He'd long ago given up trying not to offend her. The aunts seemed unsettled, and he guessed they'd all been trying to avoid her prickliness since they'd arrived.

As soon as he and Nina got to their room, Nina closed the door and leaned against it, her eyes wide. "Your mother —"

"I know."

Nina shook her head. "Poor thing. She won't let anyone in."

"Never has. No one except Dad and maybe Timothy."

"Oh, she must be scared to death.

"Don't ever let her hear you say that. In her book she's staying true to her faith. Anything else would be sinful complaining."

"I'm not sure what my role is here," Nina said.

"Why, darling, your role is to be my helpmeet," Jonathan said with a smile. As expected, Nina bristled, before finally laughing with him.

"Be serious," she said.

"Don't worry. You can't do anything right, so don't try."

"You're a lot of help."

Jonathan smiled. "Listen, I don't mean to abandon you, but I'd like to go outside a little."

"Go," Nina said. "I'll be fine."

The sunlight in Nebraska is bright. In July it can feel like the light of an interrogation. As a kid, Jonathan had found refuge from the intensity of that light in the barn. For him light had a sound, and the harsh sunlight of Nebraska was at times cacophonous. By contrast, the light in the barn was a whisper as it filtered through the old siding and the clerestory windows tucked under the eaves. At a certain time of day in midsummer, Jonathan knew, a shaft of sun entered through the haymow door and cast a dramatic spotlight on the floor near the old holding pens.

No matter how much time had passed, his first thought when entering the barn was of Karalee dancing in that spotlight the first time he'd brought her to the farm. She'd teased him that day when instead of taking her to the house, he'd taken her to the barn. He'd tried to explain to her about the barn, but he knew she hadn't ever really understood what it meant to him. She hadn't understood about the light. Almost no one did, except maybe Monty.

His father had built the barn himself with only a little help from the Mennonite community the summer Jonathan was nine. His father had wanted an untraditional barn and had used no plans except a rough sketch on a piece of graph paper. For measurement he'd used a sundial like his own father, an Old Order Mennonite, had taught him when he was a kid growing up in Ontario. That pretty well summed up things with his father. He'd never done anything conventional in his life.

In the barn Jonathan always felt the same feelings of reverence he experienced in the great cathedrals of Europe. He hadn't been a believer for almost half a century, but every time he entered that space he felt an irrational urge to pray. He felt it again now as he stood in the middle of the straw-strewn floor amid old milking stalls, unused halters, and the dusty leather tack hanging along the walls. He smelled the molding hay bales along the edges of the haymow, the dry wood of the holding pens, the ubiquitous composite of dust and grain and old manure. There had been cattle and horses, hogs and sheep, on the place when he was a boy. Now all that sheltered here were mice, spiders, feral cats, and barn swallows casting nervous shadows in their flight in and out of the haymow door. His father had gotten out of the livestock business once the markets for organic grain became more lucrative. He'd built state-of-the-art grain storage units behind the barn with fans and good air circulation, and come harvest, those would be full of organic oats and barley and popcorn.

He wandered around the barn, finding all the places he'd once hidden as a kid to avoid punishment, to dodge chores, to get away from the sun's relentless, probing light, to think. He was trying to think now. Jonathan didn't know what he'd pray for or to whom, but the urge was still there. And so was Kara-lee, forever twirling in the middle of the open floor, laughing, her red hair fanning out around her.

After he left the barn, he walked out to the pond. He wanted to see the accident site for himself, and he wasn't surprised to see several neighboring farmers and men from the church standing around scratching their asses, speculating about what had happened. One thing was clear: his father had suffered, and he'd suffered plenty. The guys down at the pond could see it, too, how the tractor had tipped and held him under, and him so afraid of water. It'd been a horrible death. No matter what anyone had told his mother.

The puzzle was why his father had been dredging the pond's edge for clay. It was clearly in service to the massive clay soldiers that lined the western side of the pond. None of the men standing around said anything about those soldiers. They all pretended they didn't exist. Typical. There was no way to ignore them, though. Larger than life-size, Jonathan had been at first a little freaked out by them, afraid maybe his father had gone senile before the accident. It was dusk, and the sun was low in the sky so that they cast long shadows across the prairie, making them eerily lifelike and forbidding. Once he got closer, though, he knew — unlikely as it seemed — they were the work of a child. His father had helped, no doubt, but Jonathan could see in the chronicle of progress a child's hand. Anna June, he guessed. Who else could it be? His father would have done anything for her, and here was the proof if anyone needed it.

He walked around the clay figures — a massive and impressive collection, given the work that had gone into each one. As he studied them, he could see how his father had developed a template for the forms. He'd used rebar to strengthen the clay and had devised a crude method for open firing. A couple hundred yards away from the figures, he saw an enormous fire pit and a large pile of cottonwood branches he guessed his father had used to create a flame hot enough to fire the figures to a bisque stage. They'd then been painted with some sort of protective coating.

The first figure had been the giveaway it was a kid's doing. Little more than three balls of ascending size, it was a snowman in clay. The figures had immediately become more sophisticated, the later ones embellished with small pieces of embedded metal, ceramic, and glass. Their sober, sightless faces were haunting as they looked soundlessly in judgment across the empty prairie. That's how Jonathan saw it, anyway. But why had his unfrivolous father gone along with this thing?

He was still puzzling over this question as he walked back toward the house, when Leroy Yoder, one of the church elders, stopped for him. "Hop in," Leroy said.

"Thanks. I'd like to walk."

Leroy frowned at this. "Come on, hop in," he said, as though Jonathan hadn't heard the first time. Jonathan knew not to argue. Out here walking when you could ride might suggest you were crazy, or worse. And still, somehow his father had managed to be his own man in the midst of all this conformity. Jonathan had to give the old man credit for that. He'd found a way to do pretty much whatever he wanted his entire life.

"You still in Boston?" Leroy asked.

"Twenty-two years."

"That right? I hadn't realized it'd been that long." Leroy tapped his hand where it rested in the frame of the truck's open window. "S'pose you'll be coming back here now to help your mom and Jeffrey with the place?" Here was a good example of the question and answer all in one.

"No, that's not going to happen."

"Oh? Your wife, I suppose. She's from back east, isn't she?"

"Yes," Jonathan said, letting Nina take the blame, knowing it'd be easier that way. He could hear it now. 'His wife's an easterner. Won't hear of him coming back.' There'd be headshaking. There'd be tsk-tsking. But they'd have their answer, and more than anything, that's what they all wanted.

By the time Leroy had dropped Jonathan back at the house, they'd moved on to safer subjects: the weather, the market this year for soybeans and corn, the war in Iraq and the troop increase planned in Afghanistan. Leroy had just been to Afghanistan with other elders from the home church. "Your dad wanted to go back to Iraq," Leroy told him now. His father had sent Jonathan a picture by e-mail in 2003, shortly after the start of the war there. In the photo his father, along with three other elderly Mennonites — a man and two women — were standing between armed American soldiers and Iraqi civilians. Jesus. What insanity.

Jonathan had wondered sometimes if it wasn't a mad religion, if it wasn't a death wish disguised as a doctrine. It was their unbelievable power to refuse, their unshakable certainty. Absolutely of one mind. They were more dangerous in their way than anyone bearing arms could ever be. Jonathan had certainly lost every conflict he'd ever had with them. Five hundred years of refusing, standing up to princes and kings and popes, fearless of the heinous methods devised to stop them. What had his own puny little love ever been against that?

JULY 8, 2009

Jonathan's son, Timothy, was the last member of the family to arrive. He came while Elsa was out with the chickens. They stood together and cried, the first tears Elsa had shed in front of another person. Once they'd recovered themselves, Timothy stood up a little straighter. "I'm going to stay as long as you need, Gram Gram. I'm sleeping on the floor in your room."

"Nonsense."

"Nope. You haven't slept alone for forever. I'm going to stay as long as you need."

"Timothy."

"My mind's made up."

The friend who had driven Timothy to the farm from Chicago got out of the car then and came to stand at the edge of the yard. He was a different-acting fellow, not one of the better influences in Timothy's life, and as he introduced his friend, Elsa saw an expression she knew well cross Timothy's face.

"Do you need a place to stay?" she finally said to his friend, and Timothy smiled.

"He's not staying."

After his friend had left, Timothy turned back to her. "Is Pop here yet?" And without waiting for her reply, he said, "Did he ask about me?"

"Timothy."

"Did he?" When Elsa hesitated, Timothy's eyes narrowed. "I knew it."

"Timothy."

He sulked for a few seconds before returning to the previous subject. "I'm going to stay for a few weeks."

"There's no need for you to disrupt your life, Timothy. I have Eddie."

"Eddie."

"He's a big help."

"I know twice as much about this farm as Eddie does."

Timothy wasn't just talking; he'd worked with Haven since he was a boy. "Timothy, your grandfather is dead. You don't have to be so brave."

At this Timothy's face fell. He looked as though he would cry again, but a noise from the kitchen distracted both of them. "Is the Hall Monitor here?" he said, referring to his aunt Kathy, who when he was younger had tried to mother him.

"Yes."

"Keeping everything in order, I suppose. And the Hessians?"

They were interrupted as Evelyn called out the kitchen window to Elsa, "We're wanting to make biscuits for breakfast. Where do you keep your lard?"

Timothy smiled. "Yep. The Hessians are here."

"Evie," Elsa called back. "You know I don't use lard. There's Crisco in the cupboard by the stove." She heard a cupboard door banging and then a faint 'thank you' as Evelyn found what she was looking for. Though unseen, Elsa knew her sisters would be rolling their eyes at the substitution. Not using lard? Who ever heard of such a thing? They'd blame their stepmother Marian again, as they always had.

Timothy was still smiling when she turned back to him. "Did they at least bring those ginger cookie thingumajiggers?"

"Lebkuchen? You know they did."

"That makes up for a lot."

Timothy picked up his things, and Elsa followed him up to her bedroom, where he unrolled his sleeping bag.

"I'm an old woman," Elsa said.

Timothy hugged her. "You're my best girl, Gram Gram."

"I'm old, and I'm alone, and I'm left with nothing in the world . . . your grandfather . . . well, you know how he was."

"I know. Don't worry. I mean it. I'll take care of you."

Elsa shook her head. She started to speak, but Timothy, looking out the window, had noticed Anna June sitting in Haven's truck. Elsa saw her too.

"She's taking it hard," Elsa said.

"I should go talk to her. Save me some of those lebkuch-whatevers when you go downstairs, will you?"

Elsa stayed at the bedroom window for a few minutes watching as Timothy got into the truck. She saw a skirmish of some kind before Timothy finally hugged Anna June. Anna June had been the tagalong baby at Jeffrey and Kathy's, a surprise when Kathy was forty-nine, long after their older daughters, Susan and Laurie, were grown. Elsa would never forget how Anna June, when she was still a toddler in diapers, had walked all the way to their house from Jeffrey's place by herself. Elsa had looked up and down the driveway that day expecting to see Kathy, but no. Kathy hadn't even noticed the baby was gone until Elsa called her on the radio. That's how it had been for almost eleven years, Anna June at their place or Celia's more often than not.

Timothy found her sitting in Grandpa's truck. The windows were rolled up. "Christ," he said when he got in. "Little Freak. It's sweltering in here. What're you doing?" Anna June didn't answer, and he farted. It stunk so bad she wanted to puke, but he rassled her to keep her from rolling down the window. When she finally opened the door, he said, "That'll teach you." Then he said, "I'm sleeping in Gram Gram's room. On the floor. You want to stay too? She shouldn't be sleeping alone." Anna June nodded. Timothy halfway hugged her. "You were the old man's favorite, you know, Little Freak." That was his name for her.

Anna June didn't want to cry again, but she felt her eyes start leaking anyway.

"Let's get out of here and go to the Dairy Queen in Seward," Timothy said. "I'll buy you a sundae. How 'bout that?"

"Okay. Should we tell Grandma we're taking the truck?"

"Naw. She won't even know we're gone."

Her cousin Timothy was her third favorite person after Grandpa and Celia. He was older than her. He was really old. But he acted like he was a kid. He was funny. He sent her letters in envelopes made out of things like magazine pages and candy bar wrappers. He sent her cds, but she didn't have a cd player, so he bought her her very own cd player. He said he spoiled her because he felt sorry for her having to live on the farm.

She always told him she liked the farm, she wanted to be a farmer, and he always said back to her, "You'll figure it out one of these days, Little Freak." He wrote, "Dear Little Freak. How is Freakville?"

He drove too fast on the back roads all the way to Seward. "I don't want to see anyone from Bethel, do you?" he said.

"No." She didn't want to have to talk to people who knew Grandpa. She felt embarrassed when she thought about people who knew Grandpa seeing her. It was morning and a weird time to be eating ice cream, but that didn't stop Timothy. He didn't even notice how the girl behind the counter looked at him.

"How's Crazy holding up?" Timothy said after they got their ice cream.

"He's all right." Sometimes Anna June didn't like to talk about Daddy.

"You know the farm's going to go totally to shit now, don't you?"

Anna June swallowed hard and blinked her eyes. She stopped eating. Timothy was right, but she didn't like him saying so.

"Maybe I ought to come back and take over things," he said. Anna June didn't laugh, but she looked up fast. "I could do it," Timothy said.

"Couldn't either."

They fought like this sometimes. That was what she meant about him being like a kid. He wasn't like a grown-up. Grandpa had wished Timothy could take over the farm. They'd tried it before, but Timothy always got bored and got into trouble. He would be good for forever, and then one day, out of the blue, he'd go nuts, and nobody could stop him. Not even Grandpa. Timothy got mean and called names and made Grandma cry. Anna June stayed out of the way when he was like that. He almost always did something Grandpa called "knotheaded," and they'd have to go rescue him. Later on Timothy would feel bad and apologize. He'd tell them he'd pay them back. He'd say he wasn't worthy of their love, and Grandma would cry again, and Grandpa would go out in the truck to check the crops or fix a fence.

"You wanna come, A.J.?" Grandpa would say at those times, and Anna June would nod and go along. They would drive and not say a word the whole way out and back, and when they came in again, Grandma would have supper on. She'd have made a chocolate pie because it was Timothy's favorite, and Timothy would be there at the kitchen table talking and making her laugh. Anna June and Grandpa would come in the kitchen door, and Timothy would smile like nothing bad had happened. He'd say, "You're missing out here. Gram Gram's telling dirty stories," or something like that, something silly, and Grandma would laugh and hit at him. "I'm most certainly not."

Anna June wouldn't ever look at Grandpa after one of those times, one of Timothy's "episodes," as Grandma called them. They were just part of life.

As soon as breakfast was over, her sisters started in. "Let's start a list, Spud," Emily said, using that infernal nickname they had for her.

"That's a good idea," Eleanor said. She brought over a notebook she'd found by the telephone and laid it and a pencil on the table in front of Elsa. "Just a list, Elsa May. What you'd like for the funeral." Elsa didn't pick up the pencil; she didn't look at her sisters.

"What was Haven's favorite hymn? Start there," Evelyn said.

"'The Old Rugged Cross.'"

"There you go."

Elsa sighed. She lifted the pencil and wrote, "'The Cross.'" Her sisters nodded, pleased smiles on their wide, empty faces. My, how old they'd grown. Who were these crones in her kitchen? Their smiling and nodding continued until they saw she'd stopped writing.

"What else?" Emily said.

"That's it. Pastor Roth will know what I want."

"Oh, Elsa." Eleanor frowned at her as if she were a spoiled child.

"Don't 'oh Elsa' me. He will. He knew Haven better than —" She didn't want to fight with her sisters today.

Evelyn picked up the pad and pencil. "This is a good start, sister. Maybe you feel like lying down a bit."

Elsa used this as an excuse to leave the kitchen. She went up the back stairs to avoid all the people gathered in the living room, but instead of going to her bedroom, she climbed the steep stairs to the attic, careful not to let anyone hear her. With each step up, she felt an easing of her spirit, a sense of freedom and quiet. At last away. At the doorway to the attic she stood for a few minutes to catch her breath and to soak up the stillness.

The windows were stiff with old paint, and Elsa had to struggle a little to get them open, but once she had, the morning air filled the room. She breathed in deeply, feeling as though she'd been holding her breath since the day before. She noticed the desiccated bodies of dead moths and flies in the bottom of the window frames and resisted the temptation to clean. Outside she heard cattle lowing in the neighbor's pasture. A small plane droned across the fields. A meadowlark trilled in the ditch beside the gravel road. Inside a wasp knocked against the window glass, trying to get out. Elsa let the light and the heat and the quiet of the summer morning seep into her bones, and she felt for the first time since she'd heard the news about Haven a small measure of peace.

Her old rocking chair was there in the corner of the attic, the chair she'd used when her boys were babies. As she sat down to rock, the old floorboards creaked, and she stopped herself, afraid someone would discover her and call her downstairs again. Beside the cot and under the knee wall was the old steamer trunk Haven had brought with him when he'd first come to Nebraska to work on his uncle's farm. It was the same trunk his father had brought with him to Canada from Russia in 1870. She felt as though their whole life together was in that old trunk. There weren't many things — she disliked clutter as much as she disliked noise — but some things a person couldn't discard.

Outside she heard the soft crunch of car tires on gravel, a brief silence after the engine was cut, and finally the slam of car doors. From the kitchen she heard Evelyn give a yoo-hoo — she was a big one for yoo-hooing — and the voice of Pastor Roth answering. Elsa would have recognized his voice anywhere, the soft lilting upward at the end of his sentences, the careful pronunciation of every word as if he were uncertain of its meaning, testing it.

The voices were muffled, and she guessed they were lowered to discuss how she was doing. Elsa realized she'd been straining to hear and settled back against the rocker. Finally, she heard the kitchen door open and close and voices raised in greeting and hospitality. She would need to make her way downstairs soon lest they start to look for her. For a while anyway, she wanted to keep the attic her secret.

The sun was already hot at 9:00 a.m. as Jonathan walked the half mile to Jeffrey and Kathy's place. He wished he'd worn a hat. In the fields across from his father's, he saw the corn was already in full tassel and starting to set ears. Astonishing. As a kid, the saying had been "Knee high by the Fourth of July." Large-scale farming was a different game now; he was glad his father had gotten out of it. Hell, his father had never really been in it. He'd been organic since shortly after World War II.

Still, his father had always kept up with what was going on around him. He'd one time told Jonathan that farming now wasn't about the farmer at all. "The modern farmer," he'd said, "is just a large machinery operator who goes to the bank each year for his farm loan and is told by the banker—who has his eye on the grain and livestock futures—what to plant where, never mind that the farmer just planted corn in that same field the year before. Pump enough anhydrous on it, regardless of the earth, and grow a super-crop. The crop specialist at the local co-op—his salary paid by the chemical company—comes out and tells the farmer what chemical to apply and how much." Jonathan remembered his father shaking his head when he told him that. "And not a single person around here wants to hear me say this. So, for the sake of a peaceful coexistence, I keep my thoughts pretty much to myself."

The ditches were thick with dock and clover, wild plum and sumac, tall phlox and switchgrass. The county had just laid new rock on the road, and it made walking difficult; large grasshoppers the size of his thumb plagued Jonathan, jumping like popcorn in the ditches and occasionally sticking to his clothes. By the time he arrived at Jeffrey's house, he wished he'd driven instead, like everyone else in the county would have.

Someone had mowed the grass, such as it was, and Jonathan guessed it had been Kathy. A few pinwheel ornaments spun languidly in a sparse bed of flowers against the house's foundation. Wooden butterflies adorned the garage door, and a bicycle he guessed belonged to Anna June had been dropped in the driveway. Jonathan climbed the cement steps. Through the aluminum screen door he saw Jeffrey lying on the couch, the volume of the TV turned up high. Although Jeffrey saw Jonathan, he didn't get up; instead, Kathy came to the door. She hugged Jonathan as he stepped inside.

Jeffrey nodded at him. "Heard you'd got in last night."

Kathy motioned for Jonathan to sit down. "You want an omelet?"

"No thanks. The aunts made a huge breakfast this morning."

"Something to drink?"

"A glass of water would be great." Jonathan sat down in a plaid lounge chair.

"You need anything else, Jeff?" Kathy said.

Jeffrey, who had been eating an omelet on the couch, wordlessly held up his greasy hands. The house was stuffy, and the open windows did little to help. Despite the heat, Jeffrey was wrapped in an orange, gray, and aqua afghan, something Jonathan guessed Kathy had crocheted.

Jeffrey looked back to his TV program, a rerun of Matlock. "You know," he said after a few minutes, "that Andy Griffith was a hell of an actor."

They watched the program together in silence until Kathy came back with Jeffrey's napkin and Jonathan's water. "Anything else I can get the two of you?" she said. Nina had commented to Jonathan in the past about the way the women in the church community waited hand and foot on everyone, and Jonathan said, "Why don't you sit down with us awhile, Kathy?"

"Oh, I have way too much to do, Jon," she said. "I'll leave the two of you to talk."

Jeffrey remained absorbed in the TV program while he finished his omelet. Finally, as he set aside his plate, he looked at Jonathan. "So, the old man's dead."

"Listen, Jeff, Mother would like us to pick out the casket together. That's why I came over this morning."

"That so?"

"She wants to be sure you aren't left out."

"That's good of her."

"I'm going to drive into town. I can pick you up in half an hour."

"I don't think so," Jeffrey said, looking as he said it every bit the invalid he was. Just as Jonathan started to look away, though, he saw something familiar in Jeffrey's eyes. It was a knowing and sardonic expression he remembered from their shared past. Their parents had never guessed the half of it with Jeffrey.

"Couldn't you at least make an effort for Mother?"

Jeffrey laughed. "Anything for Mother. That's always been your motto, right, Jon?"

Jonathan felt the air crackle between them. He took a sip of his water.

Kathy, as if sensing trouble, came back into the room. "Everything all right in here?"

"Just dandy, baby," Jeffrey said. "Jonny and Mother have come up with some half-assed scheme about the two of us going to pick out the coffin together." He laughed when he said this, and Jonathan suddenly wanted to punch him hard in the face. As if he knew what Jonathan was thinking, Jeffrey smiled.

Jeffrey had been the golden boy at Bethel High School. At sixteen he'd been set to graduate early, the star of the basketball team and an early admit to the University of Nebraska on a Regents Scholarship, where he planned to major in math. While Jonathan had been the earnest Sunday school dork, the memorizer of scriptures, the singer of duets for church services, Jeffrey had been reading for years from his secret stash of MAD Magazines and subversive comic books. As sheltered as they'd been, Jonathan still couldn't figure out how Jeffrey had always managed to know what was happening in the world outside. Jeffrey had known how to do his own thing without being found out by their folks or the church community. No one had a clue. He'd always waited until their parents weren't looking to knock Jonathan upside the head, seeming to take Jonathan's childish piety as a personal offense, hissing insults under his breath at Jonathan's attempts to please their parents —"simpleton, suck up, slope dick, numb nuts"— insults that had they been heard would have met with punishment, but Jeffrey had been smarter than Jonathan, clever and patient, capable of hiding behind a mask of innocence. If Jonathan tattled on Jeffrey, the stories he told seemed so implausible to their parents, they merely brought suspicion on him instead.

That had been the Jeffrey before, the Jeffrey who disappeared when Jonathan was ten. After that their parents discouraged him from going to the state university, sending him instead to the church school in Heston, Kansas, where he stayed for one year before returning home, marrying Kathy, and beginning the long act that had culminated in the man before Jonathan now, the

51

man who had been carried by their parents his entire adult life.

Jonathan decided not to rise to Jeffrey's bait this morning and stood up to go. He glanced again at Jeffrey wrapped in that hideous afghan and wondered if he hadn't finally punished their mother enough. "I'll stop by on my way into town, Jeff, just in case you change your mind."

"Are you leaving already?" Kathy said. "If you wait a second, I'll drive you over."

Jonathan and Kathy drove in silence the short distance back to his parents' place. After she had parked the car, Jonathan looked at her across the seat. "How can you stand it, Kathy?"

Kathy looked startled for a second before saying, "Could you help me carry in some folding chairs, Jon? They're in the trunk."

Inside Nina was helping the aunts in the kitchen. She followed Jonathan back to their room, where she told him about her morning. "You'd never guess your aunts were old women," she said and laughed in anticipation of her own story. "Did you know your aunt Eleanor volunteers at a rest home? She talks about the 'old folks' she takes care of. Jonathan, she's eighty-seven!" After a pause she added, "They're worried about your mother. She isn't coping well at all."

"She's never been like them."

"I know. But still. They're worried about what's going to happen to her after everyone leaves."

"We'll just have to give her some time," he said.

When Jonathan finally went in search of his mother, he found her sitting in a corner of the living room. Not particularly sociable under the best of circumstances, this situation would be all but unbearable for her. All these people in her house, all the noise and confusion, the lack of control. He squatted beside the chair where she was sitting. "I went to see Jeff," he said.

"I saw you'd gone over there."

"He isn't up to going with me to Polsan's."

"I'm not surprised. He'll have a relapse for sure over this, and here he'd been doing so well."

"Mother, won't you change your mind and just come with me? I don't feel comfortable making a decision about the casket without you."

"I'd rather you boys do it," she said. "Try your brother again. He can be changeable."

As she spoke, she picked distractedly at the fabric on the arm of the chair.

"What is it, Mother? Is there something I can do for you?"

"I'll be fine. I'll figure out something."

"What are you talking about?"

"Your father was a good man, the best of men, but you saw how he was. He gave away every dime we ever made."

Jonathan leaned back on his heels and looked up at her. "Where'd you get that idea?"

"I saw it. So did you. For years I saw it. Always giving to everyone else." She sat up a little straighter. "I'm not complaining, you hear. I trust the Lord will help me find a way through this."

"But Mother, that's simply not true. Dad showed me the books last time I was home. He'd invested well. You'll be more than fine, even with the markets the way they've been this past year. Dad was a good financial manager."

His mother smiled and patted his hand as though he were a delusional child. "I shouldn't have said anything. No need to worry over me. The Lord has always made a way."

Jonathan willed himself to be calm. "Once things have settled down, I'll come back, and we'll sit down together and get it all worked out. You'll see, Mother. You'll be fine."

His mother continued to pat his hand, giving no indication she'd heard what he was saying.

Jonathan stood up, noticing as he did how the gesture surprised his mother. She'd see it as an act of aggression, his ending the conversation on his terms instead of hers. "I'm going to get ready to head into town," he said. "Is there anything you need while I'm there?"

After greeting Pastor Roth and his wife, Grace, Elsa had gone back outside to check on the chickens again. She had already fed them and gathered the eggs, but being around her chickens comforted her. She'd decided this morning with all the people driving in and out, she'd leave them in their pen a little longer, and they were restless because of it. They darted and clucked, scolded and pecked at one another. Elsa scrutinized them closely as she did every day, looking for signs of injury or weakness. If they once drew blood, the flock would peck that chicken to death.

She could spend hours watching chickens. They were as entertaining as any animal she'd ever observed. When she was a little girl, Elsa had named all of the chicks her father ordered one spring. He'd warned her not to do it, but she'd done it anyway. Later she'd cried and cried when they'd slaughtered her pets. Only when Mama explained to her how the Lord had put those chickens on earth to feed people had she quieted.

Elsa had brought out with her an extra treat for Red. How she loved that old rascal. He stretched his neck and made as if to crow again, that vain creature. "Oh no you don't," she said and held out the grain she'd sweetened specially for him. Still keeping his head turned away from her, Red edged closer, watching slantwise before quickly snatching a bit of the grain and darting away. Elsa laughed, delighted again with him this morning. She felt close behind that brief bubbling up of joy the threat of tears and stopped herself. Tears would not do. No tears. They were all watching her. Without looking, she knew they were watching. Every move she made. Too much a show of grief, she'd be seen as falling apart and at risk of their stepping in and forcing her to leave this farm she loved. Too little grief, though, and they'd conclude she wasn't facing reality. The people she loved most were her greatest threat. Her very independence relied on her ability to appease them all. She couldn't trust a single one of them, except maybe Timothy.

From inside the house Elsa heard the banging of pots and pans, the running of water, and the laughter of her sisters rising above the din of the crowd that had gathered in the house. She didn't know what it was her sisters found so forever funny. Always laughing. And not a one of them with an easy life. Yet her earliest memories were of them laughing together. It had always been like this, Elsa standing apart. She'd been only seven when Mama had died, and she'd taken it hard. When Father married Marian two months after the funeral, a girl herself really, only a few years older than Evelyn, you'd have thought Father had killed Mama himself the way her sisters carried on about it. Father had told them he needed help with the house and the farm, but her sisters wouldn't hear it. Oh, they'd made it hard on Marian, that was sure, and Marian had found things in disorder.

Mama had been known for her baked goods, her quilts, her gentle spirit, her faith, her happy disposition, but not for a spotless, orderly house. It had taken Marian to point it out for them. No more sweets. No more shilly-shallying around while there were chores to be done. No more loosey-goosey. She'd had no luck shaping the older girls before they married and left home, but with Elsa she'd had almost a blank page. That's what her sisters said anyway.

Elsa gave Red one last bite of his treat. She surveyed the farmyard, glad they no longer had livestock to worry about. She had a few weeks yet to figure out the harvest. Already the farmers from the church had given her their assurances they'd bring it in for her, and she knew they would. Haven would have done as much for any of them. Eddie would stay on, too, though she didn't know how she'd pay him.

She saw Haven's truck was gone, and she wondered where it was. Every time she looked, she saw Anna June in it. She'd seen her the day before holding Haven's work gloves to her face, looking straight ahead. Kathy'd been right. Anna June was taking it hard. When Anna June wasn't in the truck, she was wandering from outbuilding to outbuilding like she couldn't believe the news, like she was looking for Haven. Anna June had spent more time with Haven than anyone else besides Elsa. Neither of them big talkers, every time Elsa saw them together they were talking, talking. She'd asked Haven once what he and Anna June found to say to one another, and he'd said with a funny little smile, "All manner of things."

The attic was hot, and there were dead flies all over. Timothy said someone needed to clean the place. "We could," Anna June said, and Timothy rolled his eyes. "Not us, Bother."

"We could do it; it'd be nice for Grandma."

He looked around. There was a tiny bed under the window, and he flopped down on it. He was way too big. He pointed to the rocking chair in the corner. The seat was dusty except where someone had been sitting. "See," Timothy said, "Gram Gram's been cleaning. She's been dusting with her ass." He laughed loud after he said that.

"Don't be mean, Timothy. I don't like it when you're mean."

He mimicked Anna June in a high voice, "Don't be mean." Sometimes she hated him.

Grandma said you should never hate anyone. You should only hate sin. Anna June couldn't help it. She hated people sometimes. She sat down in the rocking chair. Timothy turned on his back. His legs hung over the bed, and he put his hands behind his head.

"I haven't been up here since I was a kid." He looked at Anna June when he said that, back to nice Timothy. "Grandma showed me a picture one time of Uncle Zeke."

"Who's Uncle Zeke?"

"She never told you about Uncle Zeke? Her brother who died in the war?"

"The war?"

"He got shot."

"Nuh-uh. He wasn't in the war. What was he doing there?"

"Being a soldier, Freak. In the second war. What do you think?"

"But that was a sin. Grandma's brother was a soldier?"

"Yep. Great Grandpa disowned him just like that." Timothy snapped his fingers. "Didn't even cry at the funeral. Didn't even go to the funeral. Close your mouth, Freak. You look like a mutant. You never heard any of this?"

She shook her head.

"There's a lot you don't know." Timothy got up and started looking through things. "Don't just sit there. Come help me."

"What are we looking for? Grandma will get mad."

Timothy looked at her and rolled his eyes.

She got up and watched while he opened a trunk. The dust was terrible. There were old clothes and blankets. Baby things and a bundle of what looked like letters. Finally, Timothy stopped and looked around the room. "Here they are." He found two photo albums under the eaves by the rocking chair. "She's been up here looking at pictures."

They sat together on the bed, ducking their heads because of how the ceiling got low. They looked at old-time pictures of Grandma and Grandpa. Anna June had never seen pictures of them when they were young.

"Grandma was so pretty," Anna June said. For once Timothy didn't make fun. "She was more than pretty; she was beautiful."

Grandma had looked like a little girl when she and Grandpa were first married. "How old was she?" Anna June asked.

"She'd just turned fifteen."

"That's only four years older than me?"

"Duh."

They heard the door open downstairs. Aunt Eleanor called, "You up there, Elsa?" Anna June and Timothy didn't say anything. "I hear someone. Who's there?"

"It's just Timothy and me," Anna June finally said, and Timothy hit her in the side with his elbow like he hadn't wanted her to talk.

"You kids get downstairs now. Your grandma don't want you up there."

"She doesn't mind," Timothy said.

"Come on now," Aunt Eleanor said. "Don't make me come up."

Timothy and Anna June looked at each other and tried not to laugh. They couldn't imagine fat Aunt Eleanor getting up those stairs. Anna June started to get up, but Timothy stopped her. "Sit down," he whispered. Anna June shook her head. Today wasn't a good day to disobey. "Grandpa's dead," she said. "I'm going downstairs."

The house was loud and full of people. They were laughing and telling stories, and then they were crying. They were talking about Grandpa, how he had his own way of doing things, like organic farming. That was silly to them. When he still had cattle, they "followed him like sheep." Everyone thought that was funny too. Grandpa never understood why people drove cattle. "They're not very smart," he'd told Anna June one time. "They'll follow you to the ends of the earth, but they get excited and confused when people chase them. You have to be patient, that's all."

He always said he didn't want to have an argument with nature. "Nature will always win," he said. "I tithe to God of my money and time; I tithe to nature of what I grow. You've got to figure there will be loss. If you don't fight it all the time and you find a way to work with nature, you'll be rewarded." He'd say sometimes when he saw bugs on his plants, as long as there weren't too many, "The bugs need something to eat too." One of the men repeated that now, and everyone laughed and slapped their legs. "Did you ever?"

"I one time saw Haven's tractor stopped," Mr. Evers said. "I came over to see what was wrong, and there he was, lying flat on his back in the middle of his barley field. I ran when I saw that, sure there was terrible trouble." Mr. Evers stopped a minute, like he was maybe embarrassed because of the way Grandpa had died, before he finally went on. "I came right upon him, and without moving, Haven said, 'Hi, Chester.' 'You okay, Haven?' I asked. 'Why wouldn't I be okay?' Haven said. Well, I knew enough not to comment on that, so I said, 'What're you doing there, Haven?' and Haven said, 'Did you ever notice the underside of a barley plant . . . ?'"

Everyone laughed without letting Mr. Evers finish. Even Anna June had to smile. It was true. Grandpa got down on the ground and looked at things. He felt the dirt. He smelled it. He watched and he saw everything, and he had lots of his own ideas, not things he had learned from books. Anna June was laughing, and then she was crying because she didn't know anyone else in the whole world like Grandpa, and she didn't know how she was going to live without him.

And she wasn't finished building the hedge of angels. She wondered if that was why a bad thing had happened. Maybe if the hedge had been finished, Grandpa wouldn't have . . . oh boy, would Grandpa be mad at her thinking that. He wouldn't have liked that one bit. He would have said it was a sin of pride, thinking she could control the Lord like that. He'd told her once he wasn't sure if what they were doing, building the angels, was right or not. He was afraid it might be a sin of idolatry. He'd been praying about it and had decided the Lord approved of it so far, "But," he told her, "the ways of the Lord are not our ways, A.J. The Lord is mighty but He is just. We must recognize with awe his presence in nature and in all things. We can read the human condition in the history of our attempts to understand God's ways." Grandpa said things Anna June couldn't always understand. He told her she would someday.

She never heard anybody else in church say things like Grandpa said, and she never heard Grandpa say them to anyone else except to her. He told her one time, "A.J., you're the gift of my old age." And she thought what he meant was that he could speak his mind with her. She didn't know why he couldn't talk like that with other people, except that folks, church folks maybe especially, didn't like a person to say things they hadn't heard before. They liked to hear the same things over and over. That was how Anna June saw it.

Grandpa one time told her, "People aren't all that different from other creatures. If an ant tries to do something in a different way, the other ants will kill it. Makes it kind of hard for things to change much in the ant world." Anna June had laughed. That was Grandpa being funny.

As soon as Elsa came into the kitchen, Evelyn swooped toward her. "Where have you been, Elsa May? Pastor Roth wants to start planning the —"

"I'm here now, Evie. I don't need you scolding."

Elsa ignored Evelyn and headed into the living room. Throughout the day different groups of friends and neighbors had dropped in, and those who were newly arrived greeted her. Pastor Roth had been waiting patiently to talk to her. He was a frail eighty-three. His shock of white hair and Old Order chinstrap beard gave his fine-featured face and large forehead the look of a prophet. His blue eyes were still merry, and all the years fell away when he smiled at her, so that she could see again the jolly young man he'd been. Beside him his once pretty wife, Grace, smiled out of an old woman's face. She'd been sick for years, battling strange ailments of which they never spoke except in the most discreet terms. Elsa had always wondered at the secrecy, but she guessed ministers struggled with the need to balance their private lives with their church friendships.

"Elsa, my dear," Pastor Roth said. "Could we talk?"

"Of course."

"Is there a quiet place?"

Every chair in every room was occupied, and Elsa gestured toward the porch.

Pastor Roth steered her through the crowded living room and out the front door, where an old aluminum glider sat rusting. No one ever used this porch. Pastor Roth gallantly cleared away the dust. He waited for Elsa to sit before joining her. Elsa's gaze narrowed, and she noticed how the flowerbeds along the side of the house needed weeding. She started to rise, ready for the work, but sensing the spasm, Pastor Roth laid a gentle hand on her arm.

"Dear Elsa. You have such a hard time sitting still. Always did."

Elsa looked down and knit her fingers together on her lap. Pastor Roth removed his restraining hand. "Haven loved you so," he said softly. "He loved you so."

At this Elsa felt herself crumble. Tears spilled over the bottom rims of her eyes, and she couldn't seem to stop them. Pastor Roth pulled a clean white handkerchief from his suit pocket. He held it out to her, and she took it with a mumbled thank-you.

"Haven's gone home, and we're happy for him," Pastor Roth continued. "He was one of the Lord's good and humble servants. One of the best of men. We'll miss him. No one more than you."

As she continued to weep, hating her tears, Elsa felt his soothing words had been calculated to get this response. As if guessing what she thought, Pastor Roth said, "Our tears are never odious to the Lord, Elsa."

Oh, but she hated them anyway. And despite his encouragement, she wiped them away and willed herself to stop. She sensed Pastor Roth wasn't entirely pleased with her defiance. He spoke now in a slightly impersonal way, his tone less that of her old friend and more that of the minister. "Your sisters say you want a service focused on the Cross."

Elsa nodded.

"All right then. And have you given some thought to special music?"

"I'd like Charles Miller to sing 'The Old Rugged Cross.'"

Pastor Roth nodded at this, his head inclined toward her as though he were hard of hearing. She guessed it might be so.

"The Lord has given Jeffrey a new song, and I'd like Carol Janzen to sing that. Would you ask both of them for me, please?"

"Of course."

"I'd like Jeffrey to read a Scripture, but . . ."

Pastor Roth continued to nod as he finished her sentence. "We may not want to count on him in that way. It will be a difficult day for him. Who might we substitute?"

Elsa went on to tell him any of the church elders would be a fine substitute.

"I'd like Jonathan to read a Psalm, but I don't believe he'd agree to do it," she said.

"Have you asked him?"

She shook her head no.

"Will you?"

Elsa thought for a second before saying she thought probably not. Another nod from Pastor Roth. "I'll ask Eddie instead," Elsa said.

"That'd be fine." Elsa felt such restraint in Pastor Roth's answers that when he asked if there was anything else they should discuss, it startled her. She asked him what he meant.

"I didn't mean to imply anything," he said. "I was just asking."

"No. There's nothing else."

Pastor Roth hesitated. "All right." Another pause, this one longer. They heard a rumble of thunder in the west, and Pastor Roth smiled at her. "You know what Haven would say just about now?" Elsa smiled, and he went on. "He'd say, 'God's bowling.'"

Elsa laughed and shook her head. That gesture seemed to clear the air between them. Pastor Roth laughed too. "I never knew anyone who enjoyed life more than Haven Grebel, even though not everything was easy for the two of you. We know it wasn't."

Elsa felt a clutch at her heart as he spoke, and she hoped he wouldn't go on. He didn't.

She laid her hands flat on her lap, a gesture she intended to signal their meeting had come to an end. "Thank you for making the trip, Donald. It means a lot to me," she said. "Everything else in the service I leave to your good judgment. You know Haven's favorites as well as I do."

She stood up, but Pastor Roth stayed seated. He looked up at her, his blue eyes a little rheumy. "I think I'll stay here a little longer," he said. Elsa looked out again across the prairie. In the distance dense white clouds seemed to be perched on dark platforms. They moved quickly across the sky as if they had important business elsewhere.

Before going into the house, she turned to look at Pastor Roth once more. There was something forlorn about him, and she had a sudden and urgent premonition that he would not live out the year, that this would be the last time he would be in her home. She saw in him the same sadness she'd seen yesterday in Alvin Schweitzer. Everyone had a private grief. They were all affected in their own way by the loss of a fellow traveler on this earth.

The rental car was hot where it had been sitting in the sun. Jonathan turned on the air conditioner full blast and drove the long way to Jeffrey's house, looking at his father's fields along the way. Like all the area's farmers, his father was expecting a bumper crop this year. No one had ever seen anything like it. Every day since spring there'd been rain. His father had told him the weather this summer had been downright tropical.

When Jonathan pulled into Jeffrey's yard, he gave the horn a punch. It made an irritated bleating sound. He waited for a few minutes before starting to back out of the driveway and was halfway into the road when the screen door opened and Jeffrey shambled down the cement steps, a shit-eating grin on his face.

Jeffrey got into the passenger side with a grunt. "What're you waiting for?" he said when Jonathan didn't move the car.

"For you to fasten your seatbelt."

"Go, for Chrissake."

"I mean it, Jeff."

"And I mean it too. I'm not your toady. Go already."

"Jeff."

Jeffrey didn't respond and instead slumped in the seat, making it clear he was willing to outwait Jonathan. Jonathan finally put the car into gear. "You're such a pain in the ass," he said.

Bethel's main street was empty as they pulled into town. The businesses scattered about on the square had all propped open their shop doors to catch the morning breeze. On a bench outside Netler's jumble shop sat one old man Jonathan finally recognized as Jim Cornford. As a kid, he remembered old Jim Cornford always sitting on the same bench. It gave Jonathan the willies for a second, this feeling that nothing had changed since he'd left home, as though the whole place was nothing but a stage set.

He remembered then how once during the annual town parade Jim Cornford had accidently driven his car into the parade route without realizing it. Truth was, though, almost no one noticed the lapse since, unlike most town parades with marching bands and horses, a few floats and beauty queens, the Bethel parade was composed almost entirely of vehicles. One after another. Anyone with an old truck, a vintage car, or a business vehicle was in the parade, as were all the fire trucks from all the volunteer fire departments in the region. The kids' parade had been the same thing, all of the children on bicycles or tricycles or in wagons. There'd been the area Shriners too, with their tandem bikes, their motorcycles, and their miniature cars all moving in tight, intricate patterns down the street, overweight men sweating in the heat, wearing their white button-down shirts and their Shriner fezzes, some even sporting the sickle earring on their left ears. Jonathan smiled to himself remembering those parades.

In the center of the town square was a new gazebo and, lining the square, new wooden benches. He'd heard from his father there was a regular farmer's market on Saturday mornings now, and on summer evenings bands played in the gazebo. His father had mentioned these concerts, but Jonathan doubted his parents attended them.

Inside the foyer of Polsan's, the plush carpet, the air-conditioning, and the piped organ music created an alternate world. The lighting, though low, was all wrong. Too cold. In its commitment to serenity the place came off instead as unfeeling and impersonal. Jonathan looked at his watch. He and Jeffrey had been kept waiting in the foyer longer than seemed right. They'd been buzzed through a locked outside door, so they knew someone was aware of their presence. He had to wonder now about a locked door in Bethel, Nebraska. The impression it made was of locking people out, keeping their own activities a secret.

Beneath the smell of lily of the valley Jonathan thought he could smell something more acrid: chemicals and the sickly sweet smell of rotting flesh. It was a morbid thought, and he wished he could forget the image it had conjured, his father's body now subject to the macabre practices of the undertaker's dark art. Death felt like shame to him, the way the lifeless body was exposed and used in rituals Jonathan saw as keeping the living in line. If at just that moment a slight man in his early thirties hadn't entered the room, Jonathan would have suggested to Jeffrey they leave.

The man, who wore glasses more hip than what Jonathan expected to see in Bethel, extended a slim, well-manicured hand first toward Jeffrey then toward Jonathan.

"You must be Mr. Grebel's sons," he said. "I'm Brad Benson. I'm so very sorry for your family's loss." Both Jonathan and Jeffrey nodded and followed Brad Benson across a large room and up a grand staircase. "Your mother called this morning to say you'd be looking at our lower line today," he said as they climbed the stairs.

"Yes." Jonathan glanced at Jeffrey to confirm this, but Jeffrey shrugged, as if disinclined to be involved.

"We have only a few floor models in our lower price range right now, but you may look through our catalog, and if you find something you'd prefer there, we'll have it here in time for to-morrow night's viewing."

Brad Benson gestured for them to follow, and they walked up carpeted stairs to yet another floor, where he opened the door to an office furnished with a massive cherry wood desk and a matching credenza. Two light blue wingback chairs faced across the expanse of the desk, behind which two large windows were framed by light blue drapes. The whole thing was a display of the worst sort of taste, and Jonathan's judgment rose quickly and viscerally. He and Jeffrey sat down in the wingback chairs and looked at Brad Benson across the desk.

With elaborate care Brad Benson proceeded to establish the family's ability to pay for the funeral home's services. Finally, he removed a catalog from the bottom drawer of the desk and marked several pages in the back as their choices. "Just take a look," he said as Jonathan reached for the catalog. Jeffrey waved away Jonathan's attempt to share the catalog. "See if there's something in there suitable for your family's needs," Brad Benson continued.

Even before opening it, Jonathan could see the paper in the back of the catalog was thin and cheap. He was confident the models shown in that section would be pictured only in black and white, many models to a page. He opened the catalog not to the place Brad Benson had marked for them but to the front, where he saw page after page of full-color photographs display-ing caskets as lavish and ostentatious as overwrought houses or luxury cars. An entire thick catalog of caskets, updated annu-ally, Jonathan guessed. He continued to look at the models in the front of the catalog with a vague feeling of transgression, ex-hibiting curiosity when he should be limiting his feelings to the narrow corridors of grief.

He glanced up at Brad Benson, whom he found studying him with a well-rehearsed neutrality. Jonathan felt tempted to comment in some way but decided against it. Finally, he flipped to the back of the catalog, where he found things as he'd expected. He picked out a couple of models he thought possible, though they all looked alike to him, and showed them wordlessly to Jeffrey, who glanced without comment.

Later, in the showroom, he and Jeffrey encountered the same hierarchy of quality: the highest-priced caskets were located in the center of the room under recessed lights, while the less-expensive coffins lined the shadows along the perimeter. The less-expensive models weren't simply more spare or more simple; instead, they were cheaply and badly made. Jonathan felt the difference like someone had flipped him the bird.

While he and Jeffrey walked wordlessly through the showroom, Jonathan several times caught Brad Benson checking out his shoes, his watch, his clothing, eyes always darting away quickly each time Jonathan glanced at him. It was evident Brad Benson was a connoisseur of fine things, and Jonathan was unnerved by his secretive observations and what he guessed was a judgment of Jonathan's wealth and his choice now of the least-expensive coffin available.

"Our father . . . our father was a simple man," Jonathan said to Brad Benson. "He was a man who had strong beliefs . . . values, you know, in simplicity." Why was it, Jonathan wondered? How was it this Mennonite town, this town founded on the same values as his father's, should have this shop serving their dead? What had happened here since he'd left home? No wonder his mother had wanted him and Jeffrey to make this decision.

Then Jonathan saw in the center of the showroom a magnificent casket, if such a thing could truly be magnificent. Sleek stainless steel handles, a slim profile in elegant dove gray, a darker gray tweed interior. Jonathan couldn't imagine a single soul in this town appreciating this casket except for himself. It was as though it had been placed there just for him. Jeffrey noticed his interest and came to stand beside him.

"That's a beauty," Jeffrey said. Jonathan looked to be sure he wasn't ribbing him. He seemed sincere enough.

Brad Benson also noticed his interest. He smiled, and Jonathan hated how much he warmed to that approval. "You have excellent taste, Mr. Grebel," he said. "That's the finest model we have in the showroom. Brand-new this month."

"It isn't what my father would have wanted, though," Jonathan said. Brad Benson was quiet. Jeffrey fingered the fabric lining the interior. "Dad always admired good craftsmanship, though," he said.

That was true. Brad Benson waited. "How much?" Jonathan asked, knowing it didn't matter. Still, he took a step back when he heard the price. Ridiculous.

Later they were quiet as Jonathan drove back to Jeffrey's place. They didn't have a single thing in common except their mother and their not-so-happy memories of growing up together on the farm. Jonathan wanted to say something. He'd wanted to say something since Jeffrey was sixteen, but he didn't.

Every Saturday after she helped Grandma write the church history, Anna June went home and told Daddy what she'd learned. He always made fun of it. "That's one version of things," he'd say. "You have to learn to read between the lines, Spooder. Grandma likes to pretend everything's pretty."

Anna June knew what he meant about Grandma. She only liked to hear how things were supposed to be. Grandma even changed the stories in the history, things that Anna June herself knew hadn't happened that way. Grandma would change only a word or two, but it would make the story different. One of those things was about Anna June's own dad. She said he was sensitive. She said he'd been touched by the Lord. She pretended she'd never heard Daddy saying bad things, even bad things against God.

Daddy had told Anna June the real histories are never written down. The real stories are "circulated by word of mouth among those who know the truth." He said you could never trust the history that was written in books or talked about at school or in church. Anna June had thought about that a lot, especially when they went on field trips for school to museums in Lincoln or Omaha. They'd gone to the Joslyn Art Museum last year. There were a lot of paintings of kings sitting on horses during wars. They were always painting about wars. She mentioned that to Daddy when she went home. He said, "The big fish eat the little fish."

Daddy told her the church history in a different way from Grandma. At first Anna June hadn't wanted to believe Daddy's stories, but after a while she started to. That's why she started making the secret cards. Daddy told her not to spread the stories around. "These aren't for public consumption," he said. "You don't want Grandma getting wind of this. Truth is, Spooder Bug, the world can't take too much of the truth."

Anna June kept the cards for the True Secret History in a shiny purple shoebox she'd found in the garage. She'd bought note cards with lines on them like the ones Grandma used for the church history. When she was doing research for Grandma in the newspaper office or the library, she'd do research for herself too.

She'd added something new to the secret history today, something about her own family. It was a big thing. It happened with just the aunts in the kitchen making lunch. Even when they weren't talking, Anna June heard them singing to one another. "Remember this, remember that." She heard them saying things about Grandma in their singing way. They didn't understand Grandma. They worried about her because of Marian, because of how Marian had locked her in the pantry when she got upset with her. She was just a little girl, they said in their way while they laughed and washed dishes and talked about other things. They felt bad because they hadn't helped her. They should have protected her. Their father should have protected her.

And then they were really talking to each other, and Anna June wasn't listening anymore. She was eating a brownie, and they'd forgotten she was there at the table. They talked about

74

their mama, how none of the grandchildren had gotten her looks, except "Elsa's three boys." Anna June looked up. Three boys? A mistake. That's when they noticed her, and there was a pinging in the air, a silence in which they weren't talking anymore, but she could hear the singing again. They sounded like birds when they get excited and worried. The aunts were worried. They tried to pretend it hadn't happened, that it was a mistake. Anna June stayed quiet. Maybe they would talk again, but no. They were on their guard.

"Don't you mean two boys?" she finally said, and they nodded. Anna June could tell they were lying to her. Anybody could see it. They didn't like to lie.

Later she asked Timothy about it. He got a weird look on his face, not the way he usually looked, and Anna June felt something buzzing in her head. "How'd you hear that?" he said.

"From the aunts."

"What'd those stupid old ladies tell you that for?" He seemed mad at her.

Anna June told him she didn't know.

"Never mind," he said and laughed like it was nothing.

Anna June saw he was trying to joke with her, but there was still a buzzing. She asked him again to tell her.

"There are things you don't need to know." When Timothy said that, she started to cry. "See what I mean. You're just a baby." He was quiet for a few minutes. They were sitting together outside, and he ran his hand through the grass. "They're talking about Daniel," he finally said.

"Who's Daniel?" Anna June felt a shiver when she said the name.

Timothy got quiet again for a few seconds. "He was our uncle. He died."

"How?"

"That's for me to know and you to find out."

"Stop teasing me all the time, Timothy. Tell me."

"I can't, Anna June."

Timothy never called her by her name, so this got her attention. "Do my older sisters know?"

"No."

"Does Mom know?"

"Of course, stupid."

"Why won't you tell me?"

Timothy sighed. "You going to add this to your True Secret History?" he said in his mean way.

But she did add it to the secret history. As soon as she went home, she took out a new note card and wrote in her best handwriting:

Haven Grebel Family

The aunts were talking today (07/08/09) about their mama. They said "none of the grandchildren had gotten her looks, except Elsa's three boys."

Timothy told me about Uncle Daniel who died. Timothy won't tell me how he died. (How did Daniel die?!!)

When she'd finished the card, she put it in the front of the box, where she kept the cards that needed more research. It wasn't a real card until she knew all the facts.

"How'd it go at Polsan's?" his mother asked when he got back to the farm.

"We bought a casket," Jonathan said.

She looked fretful. "I suppose they'll send the bill."

"Don't worry about it, Mother. I've got it covered." Jonathan's tone was sharper than he'd intended. "I mean it," he said more gently. "I've taken care of it."

While Jonathan had been talking to his mother, he had happened to glance out the window in time to see Alvin Schweitzer come into the yard towing the tractor back from the pond. As soon as he could, Jonathan made some excuse to his mother and went outside, waving for Alvin to stop.

"Good of you to do this, Alvin," he said. "Would you mind pulling the tractor out behind the old corncrib over there?"

Alvin looked in the direction where Jonathan had pointed. "No problem," he said, though his expression told Jonathan he thought it was an odd thing to ask. But Jonathan knew his mother, and seeing that tractor would set her off. No doubt about it. She'd never forgive the thing. It'd be just like the yellow Pontiac.

He remembered how he'd begged to go to the car lot in Lincoln with Jeffrey and his father all those years ago. It had been a cold day in November, the sky as gray as the asphalt in the car lot. Nine years old, Jonathan had been so bored he could hardly stand it. Once he was there, he hadn't understood why he'd wanted to go in the first place. He had laid down in the backseat of the old car and watched the multicolored plastic flags forming the border of the dealership flutter in the wind. He remembered still the sound of those flags through the closed windows of the car and how lonely they'd made him feel.

At fifteen Jeffrey had been all about the new car. For weeks he'd been researching and sharing his findings with their father each night, wheedling for another car. He had arguments for every one of their father's hesitations, finally convincing him to buy new. That day at the car lot Jeffrey had eagerly gone from one car to the next, opening hoods and looking closely at the engines. Once he and their father got back into the old car to discuss their options, Jeffrey had spoken knowledgably about how the Pontiac was their best choice, and his enthusiasm had impressed their father.

A year later it was snowing as Jonathan watched from the window of his upstairs bedroom when the truck pulled into the yard towing the yellow Pontiac behind it. He'd watched as Mother ran out of the house without a coat into the bitter cold. The driver had gotten out of the truck but kept the door open like a shield between him and Mother. Jonathan hadn't been able to hear anything from inside the house, but he could see the man was nervous, unsure what to do, until Jonathan's father emerged from out of the snowstorm. He shook the man's hand while at the same time guiding Mother under his arm and inside his coat, where he seemed to restrain her.

After the truck had left, Jonathan watched as his father pulled his mother into an embrace and wrapped her completely inside his jacket. She submitted but only for a few seconds before she finally pushed away and turned back to the house. Jonathan knew he would never in his life forget the look he'd seen on his mother's ravaged face that day, a resolve so absolute no amount of time would ever cause her to crumble.

Jonathan had a theory that everyone had their own rock bottom, and if you ever reached it, the damage was irreversible. You'd go on living, but you'd be marked by it. That would have been his mother's rock bottom for sure. It was the end of the mother he'd remembered from before.

Elsa was irritated to see someone had been in the attic. It had to have been Timothy and Anna June. With the threat of rain later that afternoon, she closed the windows, and it was while she was closing the last window that Elsa had a terrible thought. Oh dear. Oh dear. She made her way back downstairs as quickly as she could. Careful now. Careful on the stairs. Careful. That's all she'd need was a fall. All she'd need.

Her face must have looked stricken as she entered the kitchen, for her sisters and Doreen rushed to her.

"What is it, Elsa?" Doreen said, taking her elbow and guiding her toward a chair at the kitchen table.

Elsa resisted her. "The eggs," she said. "I forgot all about the eggs from the other morning. Oh dear. I'm such a forgetful old fool."

"But Elsa, that's been taken care of," Emily said. "We already washed and boxed up the eggs, dear. Kathy helped us. She took them to Open Harvest for you yesterday." Emily gestured toward the refrigerator door. "The check's in that envelope." Elsa saw the envelope held in place by a Blue Valley Co-op magnet.

"Oh my," she said. "Thank you all." She felt her heart still knocking against her ribs. "I had such a scare."

"Elsa, you're white as a sheet. Sit down now," Evelyn said. "Are you all right?"

Doreen pulled out a chair at the table and gently took her arm again. "What can we get for you?" she said.

"Don't pay me any mind. That's not what I want. I just —" Elsa pulled herself together. "Thank you, all of you, for your hard work."

Eleanor put her arm around Elsa and squeezed. "We wouldn't want to be anywhere else but here for you, sister." Elsa felt as if a dam wanted to burst inside of her, and she knew if she started, she would never stop the tears. She stiffened and moved out from under Eleanor's embrace. Eleanor looked surprised and hurt by the gesture.

"I'm fine," Elsa said. "Don't you be worrying about me, you hear? I'm doing just fine. It gave me a scare, that's all, thinking about all those eggs going to waste like that."

"Is there something else you're worried about?" Doreen asked. "Is there something else that might have slipped all of our minds?"

"Nothing more. Please. You've already done too much. I don't know how I'll ever repay all of you."

They looked at her with expressions of dismay. "But you mustn't think in those terms," Emily said. "We love you, Elsa. We want to be here." The others nodded at this.

"You know what I want to do right now?" Elsa said, deciding on the spot how to get out of the house and out of this uncomfortable conversation. "I want to go walk around and look at the old oak grove Haven and I planted that year he came back from Virginia. That's what I want to do."

"Yes, of course. Go on," Doreen said. "You do whatever comforts you most. Would you like one of us to go with you?"

"No. Please. I'd like to be alone." Elsa left, slightly amazed to be getting out of the kitchen without anyone suggesting she eat.

Until she'd mentioned them, Elsa hadn't thought about the oaks, but it seemed like a good destination now as she left the house. She remembered all the things she and Haven had planted over the years, their whole lives spent sowing seeds in the earth. She noticed the iris plants around the foundation of the house. They were finished blooming now, but their foliage was still pretty and green. She and Haven had made a special trip one spring to her childhood home in Kansas to get some of the bulbs Marian had thinned, offshoots from the iris Mama had planted well over a century ago.

As she was thinking about the iris, out of nowhere came the phrase biological imperative. Now where had that come from? Certainly not Scripture. Where had she ever heard such a thing? It must have been something she'd read once or learned in school. Was that somehow blasphemous, thinking in such limited terms about their life on earth? Surely that wasn't right that they were only here to reproduce. Goodness no.

Maybe the oaks had been an excuse to leave the house, but now that she was out among them, Elsa was glad she'd come. She remembered how the day they'd planted all those young trees, after they'd watered them in, Haven had said, "These trees will outlive both of us, Elsa. In fifty years they'll be tall." It had seemed impossible for Elsa that day, watching those stripling oaks as they thrashed in the wind, to imagine them tall, let alone imagining fifty years into the future. And here over sixty years later they were indeed a towering grove on the north side of the house, serving, alongside a row of mature blue spruce, as shade in the summer and a windbreak in winter.

The ground beneath the oaks was slightly muddy, so she didn't go far into the grove, but still she felt the cool air under their shade, the restfulness of their hushed dark interior. She and Haven had dug the first hole for planting all those years ago with their hands together on the shovel. They'd done such things when they were first married. They were so young and so hopeful; they'd felt everything they did together had such meaning. There was no one now to remember it, except her, no one who knew the stories of their young, sweet love. She hated this sneaking low part of herself, always tempting her to self-pity — what else could it be but some part of the fallen nature? — causing her to question, to doubt God's strength, to despair for the future.

Still, the precious daily habits they'd developed after living together for so long mattered. It would be those daily habits she'd miss most. They'd found a way to honor one another and to live together a life of faith.

The morning of Haven's accident — had it really only been two mornings ago? — they'd eaten breakfast together, as always. She had paid particular attention as they'd clasped their hands in prayer the way they always did before they ate. She had noticed how old their hands looked but how after so long they still fit perfectly together. She wondered now if that morning she hadn't had a little premonition after all — if only she'd been listening — a little warning from the Lord, as she'd wondered at how quickly their life together had passed. There was no one, no one on this earth, she would have wanted to spend the years of her life with more than Haven Grebel.

Nina climbed into the truck beside Jonathan, good sport written all over her face. She smiled at him across the seat. "So what's so important that I need to go to the pond?"

"You'll see."

Nina breathed in deeply as Jonathan drove into the pasture. She put her arm out the window. "I do like these wide-open spaces. The sky here! It makes me feel so free."

They had been driving in silence through the pasture when Jonathan felt Nina sit forward and peer through the glass. "Good Lord," she said and looked at Jonathan. He nodded. "Good Lord," she repeated. She continued to look out the window as she asked, "What is that?"

"It's what I wanted you to see."

Nina was quiet until they reached the pond, where Jonathan parked the truck on the side opposite the soldiers. He counted them now: nineteen. They were every bit as impressive today as they'd been the evening before, and together they formed a formidable wall along the eastern side of the pond.

Nina got out and walked to the edge of the water. Jonathan leaned against the truck and watched her. When she turned to look at him again, he said, "You see now why I thought you'd be interested?"

"Who did this?"

Jonathan shrugged. "It had to have been Dad and Anna June."

Nina walked around the pond to the other side, where Jonathan watched as she circled each soldier, taking in every detail, just as he had the day before. He saw her shake her head at the spectacle before she finally shouted at him across the pond, "This is stunning."

Jonathan remembered from the day before that the soldiers had no eyes, yet from where he stood across the water from them their faces had an eerie, all-seeing aspect. He felt himself shiver slightly. Even from this distance he could see how each soldier was distinct. From the stylized draping of their uniforms to the sandal-shod feet, it seemed no detail had been overlooked.

Nina came back to stand beside him. "I would never have guessed Anna June and your father could do something like this."

"Who else could it be?"

"I believe you; it's just so unexpected." She paused to look at them again before saying, "They remind me of Egyptian funerary statues."

Now that Nina said it, Jonathan could see the influence. "Anna June must have seen a picture somewhere."

When they got back into the truck, Nina said, "It makes me look at her in a completely new way." She talked the rest of the way to the house about how the talents of a girl like Anna June were being wasted in a place like this. Jonathan cringed a few times at her characterization of Nebraska as a backwater state, a place that stunted creativity and encouraged conformity, but he didn't argue with her.

Anna June tried to stay out of the house. She didn't like to see so many people. When Nina found her in the farmyard, she sat right down on the ground beside her. "Jonathan showed me your soldiers," Nina said after a while. Soldiers? That showed you how much they knew. Anna June didn't say anything. She wasn't sure she liked Nina. "They are yours, aren't they?" Nina said. "Jonathan guessed you'd made them. He took me out to the pond today. They're exquisite, Anna June."

Anna June didn't look at Nina. She saw bones behind her teeth. The words sounded like bones hitting her teeth. She talked too hard. "We think you're a special girl, Anna June. I wish we could help you get into a special school so you could develop your skills."

That got Anna June's attention. "I'm not retarded," she said. "I'm different. Everyone says I'm different, but that doesn't mean I need to go to special ed."

Nina laughed, bones and sticks on her teeth again. "Oh dear no, Anna June. I didn't mean it that way at all. You misunderstand me. There are programs for gifted children like you, children without opportunities in regular schools."

Anna June had stopped listening. Nina and Jonathan didn't come around the farm. They never came. Or sometimes they came but not a lot. They meant trouble for her. She didn't want to be around them. Jonathan had fallen away, Grandma had told her. Nina wasn't even a Christian; she was a Unitarian. Nobody talked to Anna June about Nina and Jonathan. Her mom and dad didn't say anything. Grandma didn't say anything. Only Grandpa sometimes. He said they'd made mistakes with Jonathan —"And your father," he always added. He never said what the mistakes were, only that he felt bad about it.

Elsa was deadheading the flowers along the side of the house when Nina joined her. A tall, big-boned gal, Nina seemed to sprawl a bit. She took wide steps and swung her arms vigorously. She had a wide smile and large, straight teeth. Her thick, blonde hair was held up by something that looked like a chopstick. She surprised Elsa when she knelt down and started working quietly beside her.

"Do you and Jonathan have a garden?" Elsa asked.

"We have several flower beds and an herb garden." She looked up at Elsa. "You should come visit us. You'd be welcome to stay as long as you'd like."

Elsa nodded. She and Haven had visited Jonathan only once in Boston, shortly after he'd moved there. It had been a disastrous trip. Jonathan was gloomy the entire week of their stay, as though embarrassed by them. He'd acted like they were inconveniencing him, and without ever discussing it, she and Haven had decided never to return.

"Tell me about how you and Haven met," Nina said, interrupting Elsa's thoughts. When Elsa didn't answer immediately, Nina said, "Is it hard for you to talk about it?"

"I guess it's been a long time since I've told that story, is all," Elsa said. Nina waited. She seemed intent on hearing it. Elsa straightened her back for a minute before bending to her work again. "I was just a girl," she said finally. "When I first met Haven, I wasn't even fourteen years old. He'd come down to a youth revival in Kansas, where I lived."

"So, did you like him right away?"

"Oh goodness, yes. All the girls liked Haven. There was something about him, even when he was a young man. He'd just turned nineteen that year."

"Did he like you?"

Elsa hadn't thought about it for a long time, and she felt herself smile at the memory. "That's the thing. He did like me. He chose me. There were lots of older girls who would have gone with him, but he chose me. It was the first time I'd ever been singled out in any way. I couldn't believe it when he started paying such attention."

"So you started dating?"

"No, it wasn't like that then. He started writing me letters after the revival." Elsa paused before adding, "That is, until my father found them."

Nina didn't say anything, but her quizzical look invited Elsa to go on. "Father intercepted them without telling me. It nearly broke my heart when Haven's letters stopped coming. I thought for sure he'd lost interest in me. After all, I was just a girl, and he was already a grown man at the time."

"You must have been furious with your father when you found out about the letters."

Elsa looked at Nina. "He was my father. It wasn't my place to be furious about a decision he'd made." She bent back to her work again, before adding, "But I'll admit when I found out he'd kept those letters from me, I was upset for a while."

"Then what?"

"The next year Haven came back to the youth revival again. I saw him over on the men's side of the church. He was a big man, so it was easy to pick him out. He caught my eye, and I felt something like an electrical charge pass between us." Elsa laughed softly. "He found me later during lunch and told me he was sad he hadn't heard back from me for so long, and that's how I found out about the letters."

Finished with her work, Elsa stood up and looked toward the horizon. That had been a long time ago, another life. She stopped talking, but she remembered vividly how after the revival that year Haven came to the house to visit her father, how he and Father talked together in the living room with the pocket door closed so Elsa couldn't hear a thing. It had seemed like hours later when Father finally came by himself into the kitchen, where Elsa was helping Marian with supper. Elsa had stopped what she was doing when she saw Haven wasn't with him. Father had an odd little smile on his face, a smile like she'd never seen before.

"Your young man," he said, and Elsa's stomach pitched in anticipation of what he would say next, "isn't lacking in confidence." Given Father's way, Elsa hadn't been sure if this was criticism or praise. She didn't say a word as she went back to tending with extra concentration the chicken frying in the cast iron skillet, afraid for what was to come.

"I gave him my blessing to write to you, Elsa, but I also gave him to understand I'll be reading those letters." Father paused, and Elsa saw him exchange a look with Marian. "He wants to marry you," he said, and at this Elsa's head shot up. She hadn't even been able to pretend not to be surprised. Married? Father went on like he hadn't noticed her reaction. "I told him we'd see once you were fifteen." Again to Marian, he said, "He's got good prospects, that one does. He's arranged with his uncle to be paid in land rather than wages, and he'll own a quarter section this time next year. He's got his eye on another quarter section after that." Father had chuckled then. He'd always been impressed by prosperity even as it eluded him all of his own life, and Elsa had heard in that chuckle his reason for approving things with Haven.

Nina stood up and brushed her hands against her pants. "So, how did everything get resolved with your father?"

"Oh, I hardly remember such things now," Elsa said. "The Lord intended Haven for me, and everything worked together for the good."

He'd been putting off going into his father's workshop. If the barn was a cathedral, the workshop was the monk's cell. It was not so much hushed as breathless, a space so personal and intimate that it felt as though his father's living spirit was still there, this space as much a body for that spirit as the physical body had been. The fact of it hit Jonathan so viscerally as he entered, he felt dizzy and had to sit down on a wooden barrel in a dim corner. He couldn't name the dread he felt, only that it seemed as if he'd been taken up and thrown down by a force far more powerful than himself. He remembered the Old Testament story of Jacob wrestling with the angel, and he felt as though he were wrestling something with a stamina that would outlast his, something that would inflict a wound on him. He'd be marked just as Jacob had been marked by his encounter with the angel.

His father's spirit was loose in the world now, liberated from the local and the specific, looming everywhere and absolved at last of all earthly grudges. The anger Jonathan had felt toward his father all these years seemed futile to him, sniveling and ridiculous. He'd never experienced anything like this feeling before. He'd always been able to locate himself in terms of his stance against home and church. For years he'd seen himself as set apart from the past, but he felt now as if he'd lost his bearings, as if he'd been cut loose from the earth itself and was bobbing about in space without mooring. He thought maybe this was what some people meant by grief. It surprised him. It wasn't what he'd expected at all, the bewilderment of it, the way he felt frightened and diminished by the totality of the loss. His father was irrevocably gone, and yet he'd never felt his presence so fully.

After a long time of sitting in this stupor, Jonathan came back to himself, back into the present again, where he surveyed the workshop. His father's tools were all in their place. Typical. His father took good care of things. They were old, many of them tools he'd brought with him from Canada when he'd first started working on his uncle's farm. The wood handles had been replaced on a few over time, but the steel was still original. His father had taught Jonathan respect for things, what he'd called "good stewardship."

Jonathan approached the workbench, where he picked up the tools one by one, and observed as he did how they didn't fit his hand. A man's tools came to conform to his own hand. He wished suddenly he could take something back with him to Boston, and he started lifting each tool with that intent, mimicking the gesture of its use. What did he want? The hammer? The vise grip? The hatchet? The crowbar?

As he replaced a wrench, he noticed under the workbench three empty drywall buckets filled with incomprehensible junk: broken crockery, bits of glass, and pieces of metal. Uncharacteristic of his father, the contents made no sense to him, and Jonathan feared again there had been dementia before the accident, until he realized these were the materials his father and Anna June had used to create the mosaics in the clay soldiers' armor. Jonathan wondered once more at the extent of his father's participation in that project. Why? And more churlishly, why had he done this frivolous thing for Anna June, when he would never have done such a thing for Jonathan or Jeffrey?

As much as Jonathan had wanted a tool a few minutes earlier, he now no longer cared. He didn't need any tools. The truth was, his father shouldn't have needed most of them either. What had the old man been thinking anyway, eighty-five years old and still farming full-time? Carrying Jeffrey's pathetic ass all these years? Still going on dangerous missions with the Mennonite Central Committee? Using the tractor to dredge for clay by the pond in service to a childish whim?

Jonathan continued to brood as he opened the top four drawers of the workbench and studied their contents. When he tried to open the first drawer in the next row, it stuck. He jostled it, assuming one of the tools had wedged against the opening. As his efforts failed, he took the crowbar from the pegboard and tried to gently pry the drawer free. When this attempt also failed, he applied more pressure. Still nothing. Finally, he leveraged all his weight behind the crowbar, not letting up even as the drawer's face began to splinter. The noise of the breaking wood infuriated Jonathan, and he kept on until he'd destroyed the drawer. Unsatisfied even with that damage, he reached into the opening and pulled from it socket wrenches, graduated drill bits, Phillipshead screwdrivers, and Allen wrenches, and still he wasn't satisfied. It wasn't until every drawer in the workbench was empty that he saw how he had hurled his father's tools about the room, tools his father had kept carefully his entire life.

Jonathan saw in this destructiveness how his behavior, how he himself, was an affront to this space, to the purity of its purpose, to the spirit of calm and order and prayerful service of its long occupant. He had desecrated his father's orderly life, made light of his deep and true faith. With that realization he fled from the workshop as if he were fleeing for his life. Only after he'd reached the yard was Jonathan relieved of the overwhelming presence of his father's disapproving spirit. He bent at the waist, panting with the emotional exertion as much as if he'd exerted himself physically. He finally stood up and looked around, hoping no one had noticed what he'd done.

While he'd been in the workshop, thick clouds had developed across the sky, completely blocking out the sun. In the distance a flash of lightning lit the curtain of clouds.

On her way to the barn Elsa noticed Jonathan in the workshop. He had taken out the table saw and was fitting a piece to the front of the workbench. She didn't want to disturb him, whatever it was he was doing, and went the long way around, ending up out by the old corncrib.

Elsa hadn't been behind these outbuildings in decades. She supposed it was the same for Haven. There must have been cupboards and closets where he never looked, whole parts of one another's daily lives in full view of the other but never seen. This wasn't profound. Elsa didn't want to make much of it, but it gave her a peculiar feeling anyway.

Old bridal wreath spirea and lilacs grew wild back here, where the foundation of the original homestead had once stood. It was shady and peaceful, away from the furor of the house. She walked through rusting farm implements, a little surprised Haven had kept some of them when they were no longer of use. That's when she saw the tractor. THE tractor. It had been parked behind the corncrib a little apart from the other retired farm machinery. Seeing it there like that gave Elsa a shock.

She guessed Eddie had thought to put it out of sight. That

gesture of kindness touched her. And here that tractor — a narrow-front Farmall H — had always been her favorite, the first tractor she and Haven had bought together. They'd been so proud of it, kids that they were, and she'd never forget how, after they'd brought it home, Haven had taken her for a drive in the pasture, she beside him leaning against the fender. He'd driven it a little too fast, enjoying her squeals begging him to slow down. He'd teased her later, "Slow down now. I mean it, slow down," so that she'd had to laugh at herself hearing him mimic her that way. They'd driven all the way to the pond that day, and she'd brought a blanket and a hamper of food, and they'd had a picnic there. She felt a little flushed thinking about how they'd been when they were young and first married, how they'd acted with such abandon. Those had been sweet times, though. Until now she'd forgotten how they used to do things like that. In later years they'd kept a little rowboat there for the boys. They hadn't needed fancy things to have fun. She turned away from the tractor, suddenly unable to stand the sight of it.

Large cumulous clouds rolled across the sky like a caravan of lumbering animals. In the distance she heard a rumble of thunder. There'd be rain again before the end of the day. She watched as a flock of sparrows flitted from the telephone wires to the tops of the Chinese elms bordering the house. Red-winged blackbirds perched uneasily on fence posts, and in the pasture grass she heard the fluting of the meadowlarks. The birds seemed nervous today, as if sensing a storm. She thought how not one of those birds fell but that the Lord took notice. Out here, away from the house, she felt the Lord's presence most fully. He'd been her truest friend all the years of her life. He wouldn't fail her now.

"Gram Gram." Elsa hadn't heard Timothy until he was beside her. "Sorry to scare you, Gram. What are you doing way out here?"

She gestured toward the tractor. "Oh," Timothy said. Elsa had been standing, but now she sat on the edge of an old wagon tongue. Timothy sat down across from her on the grass, resting his back against the weathered boards of the corncrib. He picked a stem of foxtail growing beside him and idly stripped the seeds away.

"When I was a kid, I used to play out back here."

"I didn't know that," Elsa said. "I wouldn't have thought it was very safe."

Timothy smiled. "That's why I never told you." He looked around at the rusting farm implements. "I used to pretend these were dinosaurs."

Elsa laughed. "You had such an imagination when you were a little boy."

They sat quietly for a long time, both of them watching as the clouds began to sag, bellies dark and heavy with rain.

"You know what you're going to do now, Gram?"

"Oh, Timothy, I'll figure it out. The Lord always takes care of His own, and I have to trust Him." Timothy nodded, and she went on. "I'd like to stay here on the farm, but if I have to give it up, and I can't afford one of those places in town —"

"Those old folks' apartments?"

"Those."

"Gram, you can't live there. What would you do with your chickens?"

She wished he hadn't mentioned the chickens. She didn't think she could quite manage yet the idea of being without them. "If I can't afford one of those places," she continued, "maybe I can go back to Heston, be the dorm mother at the college."

"Gram Gram."

"Well, what would you have me do, Timothy?"

Timothy picked another stem of foxtail and set about stripping it of its seeds. Elsa watched him silently, and when he looked up, he seemed to be amused by something. She never knew with him. He was changeable, and she was never sure what direction his mind would take. His moods could turn faster than anyone she knew. When he was a boy, he could get settled into one of his moods and refuse to talk to her or Haven for days at a time. Not that she blamed him. It shamed her still to think about how Jonathan had behaved when Timothy was a child. No matter that Timothy was thirty-five years old; he'd always be her baby. There was a special bond between them. She'd never forget how he sobbed when he was a little boy those times when Jonathan had made him leave the house so suddenly he didn't have a chance to take along his favorite things.

In those days, when Jonathan came, they never knew for sure how the visit would end, if he would take a wild hair and accuse Elsa and Haven of indoctrinating Timothy and leave with him — shouting on his way out the door that they were trying to steal Timothy from him — or if he would take off early one morning without so much as a good-bye, leaving Timothy to spend another few months in their care.

It got so finally Timothy kept a little bag packed, and when Jonathan came, he'd put that bag by the door so he'd be ready if his father up and decided to leave with him on the spur of the moment. It had broken Elsa's heart a little every time she saw that bag, the way Timothy was shuttled back and forth and how he'd tried to be prepared.

"Gram Gram. Let's go back in." Timothy was standing now, and he held out his hand to help her up as he glanced toward the sky. "There's rain moving in."

"My, I'm stiff," she said, taking his hand.

"I wouldn't wonder. You've been perched on this wagon for half an hour. Time to go back inside and talk to your friends and admirers." Elsa harrumphed at this. "They'll have a search party out after you if you don't get back soon."

As they walked to the house, Elsa took Timothy's arm. He snugged her closer. "You know, you could always do what Dan Ebersbacher did," he said, and Elsa glanced up to see the same amused expression she'd seen earlier. She smiled at him, and he continued. "You could borrow a little from the church. You've got access to the quilt funds."

Elsa stopped. "Where ever did you hear such a thing about Dan Ebersbacher?"

Timothy's face closed, and he shrugged. "Everyone knows it."

"They most certainly do not."

"Never mind, Gram Gram. I was just joking. You know that." Timothy took her arm and tucked it back in his. Elsa reluctantly moved on, but she couldn't stop thinking about what Timothy had said. Where on earth could he have heard that story? There were only a couple of families who knew about that situation. It had been kept quiet all these years.

Jonathan was gone from the workshop when they walked past. "Looks like Pop finished his little project."

"What was that all about?"

Timothy smiled. "Making a few repairs —" He was interrupted by a flash of lightning and a crack of thunder, followed by the first slow drops of rain. They hurried and made it inside just as the storm broke.

Emily was at the kitchen sink peeling potatoes. "Just watch how that rain's coming down," she said.

Elsa and Timothy sat down at the kitchen table. "I can't get enough of these," Timothy said to no one in particular as he reached for several lebkuchen. "I never get these at home."

"I should give you the recipe," Emily said.

"Now there's an idea." Timothy's cheeks bulged, and Elsa was

tempted to scold, like she had when as a boy he ate too greedily
—"Slow down!"—but she held her tongue. She was still thinking about what he'd said about Dan Ebersbacher and had a terrible suspicion about where he'd heard that story.

"Timothy, tell me the truth," Elsa said, lowering her voice.
"That story you mentioned earlier, did Anna June tell you that?"

Timothy's mouth was full, and he shook his head, but she noticed the way he deliberately avoided her eyes. She didn't back
down from the question and continued to look at him as he
chewed. "Tell me," she said.

He sighed. "Gram."

"Tell me."

"It's nothing, Gram Gram. It's just kid stuff." Elsa waited.
"She doesn't mean anything by it. Anna June said she heard some
stories while she's been helping you with the church history."

It was true Elsa had mentioned there were stories they couldn't
include in the official community history, but she'd never elab-
orated on those stories, and she knew she had been especially
careful never to betray confidential matters to Anna June. She
cast her mind back. Had she ever mentioned anything to Anna
June about the situation with Dan Ebersbacher?

Timothy repeated, "It's nothing, Gram." He added then,
"She's just playing, you know. She's made a few cards of her
own, that's all."

At this Elsa felt her skin prickle.

"She calls it the True Secret History," Timothy went on, laughing then with real merriment until, sensing Elsa's dismay, he hurried to say, "Honestly, Gram, don't get wound up about it. It's
nothing. She's just a kid. You know how kids are."

"But where could she have heard such stories?" Elsa asked,
fearing the answer.

Timothy finished chewing. "Gram Gram, you taught her how

to do research. You can't be surprised if she got curious about things and found out stuff on her own."

"I find that hard to believe."

"Why?" Timothy asked, and his impertinence troubled her.

As they'd continued to talk, Elsa was seized with panic at the thought of those cards. They could only be the worst stories, the stories that would do the most harm to the community. She couldn't imagine how much it would hurt the church if the congregation was to learn about Anna June's cards — her "secret history," as she called it. What a disaster it would be if the most shameful stories about the past were to be broadcast.

Elsa took hold of Timothy's arm. "You've got to find those cards for me, Timothy." When he didn't respond, she gripped his arm more tightly. "They have to be destroyed. You understand that, don't you?"

"Gram," Timothy said again.

"I mean it, Timothy. Find them for me. If it's the only thing you do for me in this life, find those cards. Go now." Timothy looked out the window at the pouring rain. "Please," she said, and with a sigh he pushed his chair away from the table.

"Thank you, dear Timothy. Thank you. Take the truck."

She watched as he left through the kitchen door. The storm had picked up, and she listened past the wind and rain for the truck to start. She listened to it as it rattled down the driveway, imagined it skidding a bit in the mud before it turned onto the gravel road toward Jeffrey and Kathy's house. She urged Timothy on. What could Anna June be thinking? She was like a baby with a bomb. Elsa felt every muscle in her body tense as if waiting for disaster. What if that child had talked to people about what she knew? Elsa knew very well Anna June told that silly friend of hers everything. What if Celia talked to her parents? Or to her other friends? All the most closely guarded secrets of the church community, the things no one would want to have known, spread by the talk of careless children. Please, Jesus, let Timothy find those cards.

As she turned back to the kitchen, she caught sight of Haven's barn coat hanging on its peg just inside the door. She still halfway expected to see him coming in, shaking the rain off himself, and laughing about being caught in the storm. What she wouldn't give to see him come in that way again. He'd have noticed the yard full of cars and see all the food on the counters, the living room full of people. He'd be wearing that puzzled expression she knew so well—one eyebrow cocked and a half smile—as he said, "What's the occasion?" happy to see so many friends and loved ones together at one time.

She'd done the work of writing down the stories her dad told her. They were her cards. Nobody could have them if she didn't want them to. She wasn't trying to hurt anyone. Anna June didn't want to think about what Grandpa would say to her about it. They were her cards.

And that skunk Timothy. That dirty skunk. He'd gone and told on her. She'd shown him the secret history because he didn't believe her about Dwayne Miller and the quarter section he used to own over by Highway 34. All Anna June had said was, "He stole that land from his own mother."

"Did not," Timothy had said. "What are you talking about, you little freak? Why are you lying like that?"

"I'm not lying. My dad told me. He took the land, and they had to go to court and everything." Timothy had still looked at her like she was making up things, so she took him to her house and showed him the box with her cards.

"You little sneak," he said after he'd looked through them.

"I'm not a sneak." That had hurt her feelings. "Daddy told me the stories. He said Grandma wouldn't write them in the history, so I made my own cards. They're secret cards. You can't tell anyone about the secrets."

"Do you know how much trouble you'd be in if Gram knew about this?"

When he said that, Anna June had felt like her head was going to float away. "My dad told me."

"You're family, moron. You can tell your family things, but you can't let on you know, and you can't write them down where people can find them. You're such a stupid kid."

That was twice in one day he'd called her stupid, and Anna June was darned tired of it. She stopped talking to him until he said, "Come on, Little Freak. Don't be mad." He tried to get her to like him again like he always does because there's something wrong with him, so that he can't act like a grown-up. He'd even said so himself one time. "I know I'm not right," he'd said. But he didn't even try to act right. Like telling Grandma about the cards. That was uncalled for. He told Anna June it was an accident, but she didn't believe him. She didn't believe him for one minute.

Anna June had never seen Grandma so mad. When she rode in the truck back to the house with Timothy, Grandma pulled her into a corner. "Anna June," she said, "you've done a hurtful thing going behind people's backs like this, and I'm disappointed in you. If you bring me the cards and let me destroy them, we'll never speak of it again. It'll be water under the bridge."

Anna June was glad she'd hidden the cards after Timothy had been so mean to her about it earlier that day. She wanted to obey Grandma. She really did. But she couldn't. She felt like she couldn't breathe when she thought about it. They were her cards. Nobody else's.

"Daddy said I could keep them," she said, even though he hadn't really. He didn't even know about the cards. "Daddy says it's all right. You can't tell me what to do."

That's when Grandma got boiling mad. Her face turned red.

Her mouth got hard. Anna June stepped back. She thought Grandma was going to whack her good. She'd never been hit before except by her older sisters and Timothy and some kids at school. She didn't want Grandma to hit her.

"I'm not going to strike you, Anna June," Grandma said. "I think you deserve to be punished for your behavior, but it won't be that way. Remember this. God knows what you've done. He'll mete out a just punishment, but until you repent, you are outside the Lord's grace, and I cannot look upon you until you've made yourself right again with the Lord. And if you divulge those stories, you'll have to live with your sin and with the damage you inflict on the community. And don't you dare tell lies on top of it, young lady. I know very well your father wouldn't have approved of this."

Anna June felt bad. Grandma only used big words when she was really mad. But Grandma was wrong about Daddy. He did approve of it. There were a lot of things Grandma didn't know about him. Anna June ran outside in the rain and up to the haymow. Later that creep Timothy came sneaking up the ladder, trying to act all nice like he thought he was cute. "Oh Annie June. A.J. Oh, A.J."

"Don't call me that." That's what Grandpa had called her. Only Grandpa.

He ignored her. "A.J.," he said again.

She picked up a hayfork that had been leaning against the wall. "Leave me alone," she said. "Get out of here."

Timothy laughed at her. He could take her down in no time, but she shook the hayfork at him again. "I mean it, Timothy." And she did. She'd have hit him over the head with the fork, except she heard Grandpa's voice telling her to calm herself. She sat down on a hay bale and ignored Timothy. Before he climbed down the haymow ladder, he said to her, "Anna June, I really am sorry. I didn't know it was going to get so out of hand with Gram Gram." He scratched his forehead. "I'm going to get my act together one of these days. I really am." That was no good, though. They couldn't be friends anymore. Her mom always told her it wasn't right that she spent so much time with Timothy. Her mom thought he was weird. Last time Timothy was home, her mom had said, "He's a troubled person, and I don't think he's a very good influence for a little girl." When Anna June had asked her why, her mom had gotten a dumb look on her face. Anna June hadn't liked how she looked. "You don't know him," Anna June had said, except now Anna June saw her mom had been right. There was something bad about Timothy.

Anna June had been thinking about things Nina had told her earlier that afternoon. One of the things Nina said had gotten Anna June's interest. She'd been talking about how people around the world made crafts. "When artisanal artists —" Nina had said, and Anna June had interrupted her to ask, "Why is r teasin' l?" "What?" Nina had said. She'd looked confused, and then she'd smiled. "No, it's a word. A-r-t-i-s-a-n-a-l. Artisanal. As in, artisan. It means 'craftsperson.'"

She'd told Anna June how these artisans worked within traditions handed down over time. "They have standards within the tradition that approach perfection. Now obviously, this isn't necessarily considered art, but —" and Nina had smiled when she said this. Anna June had liked how she'd smiled. "In many cultures the artisan is uncomfortable with perfection, and they have a practice of introducing an error into their work. They don't want to compete with God." Actually, Nina had said "their gods," but Anna June figured since she wasn't a Christian, she didn't know there was only one God. "This flaw is interesting because it's entirely subjective. It's unlike the standard established by tradition, so it's in this humility flaw — that's what it's called—that we see evidence of the individual personality in the craft, the beginning of art. Do you understand what I'm saying?"

"I guess," Anna June finally said, because she sort of understood and she sort of didn't, and she didn't know why Nina was talking to her about these things anyway. But then Nina mentioned the angels—she still thought they were soldiers—and how they were art because each of them was an interpretation of the template.

It made Anna June think about how she and Grandpa had decided to use bits of broken glass and dishes and pieces of metal to make them better. They'd decided from the beginning the angels wouldn't have eyes. They didn't want them to look like humans, and if they had eyes, Anna June had thought they would look like they were. The angels weren't blind; they saw everything. "Angels see the world above and the world below." That's what Grandpa had said. "They see the Nebraska prairie, and they see the heavenly plains." Anna June had believed the angels would guard the water and that they'd guard the family.

Earlier in the day Elsa had watched how Nina pitched in to help her sisters in the kitchen. They acted like they were old friends, as if they'd known one another all their lives, when in fact her sisters didn't know Nina at all. Elsa's sisters had been teaching Nina the words to old hymns, and now Nina was teaching them what she called "protest songs." They were singing together as they worked. None of her sisters was lazy. Elsa would give them that. And Nina didn't seem lazy either. Still, as Elsa watched all of them, she had to question the worth of some of their work. They seemed forever to be moving things from one place to another with no clear sense of order.

Now as she sat at the table making a list of people who'd brought food so she could send thank-yous after the funeral, Elsa asked, "Why didn't you ever have any children, Nina?"

Nina laughed like the question embarrassed her. Elsa couldn't understand why. Most natural thing in the world, having children. She waited, and finally Nina said, "It just never worked out for me, I guess."

Elsa nodded. An idea had been forming. "You've taken a liking to Anna June, haven't you?"

"I have." Nina looked at Elsa as if waiting for her to go on. Elsa said nothing further, though she noticed her sisters exchange one of their glances.

Anna June's betrayal was a big problem. She was a menace to the community. Cards or no cards, her interest in the wrong things was of grave concern to the community. Elsa had at first mourned Jonathan's leaving, but over the years she'd come to see the Lord's greater wisdom in keeping the community safe from those who meant it harm. Hard as it was for her to admit, Anna June's transgression set her apart. She was a danger to the whole.

Elsa had first enlisted Anna June's help with the community history after she'd discovered her out behind the barn pacing back and forth preaching. Imagine it, a little girl like that preaching, and not at all like the Mennonite ministers. She could hear her still, "Do you believe in the power of the Lord? Do you believe in Christ crucified? Do you believe in the wiles of the Devil? Do you believe in the sanctification of the saints?" Where ever could she have heard such preaching?

Elsa had scolded Anna June. "You know girls can't preach."

"Why not?" Anna June had asked, and that questioning had bothered Elsa. What notions got into the minds of children.

"Because God said so," Elsa had told her, and from that day on began her campaign to keep Anna June busy, to instruct her on the right path for her life. Elsa had needed help with the church history, and Haven had needed a helper around the farm. Elsa couldn't blame Jeffrey for the gaps in Anna June's instruction, but Kathy needed to do better.

Elsa looked out through the screen door at the rain. Inside the humid air fogged the windows. She worried the rain would make things worse for Jeffrey. He so disliked gray weather. It was no surprise to any of them he'd taken to his bed. All he'd need would be to hear about Anna June acting up. He hadn't been able to come to the house yet, but Elsa was hoping he'd come later that evening. Evenings were always a little better for him. There were questions about whether or not he would make it to either the viewing or the funeral.

Jeffrey had always been a sensitive boy, and the Lord had laid such beautiful songs on his heart. She'd used some of her egg money a few years ago to help him make a CD. Haven never knew about that money. She'd always kept a little tucked away in a Kerr jar above the stove, emptying the jar into an account in the bank for just such a day as this, the way Marian had taught her to do. It wasn't much money, but Elsa was glad for it now. It was all she had in the world.

Jonathan found Nina reading in their room. "Let's get out of here," he said. She looked up from her book and toward the window, where outside the storm still raged. "I need a drink."

"Now you're talking," she said. She closed her book and slipped on her shoes. They took umbrellas from the kitchen porch and ran to the car, both of them soaked by the time Jonathan had unlocked the car, all the while grumbling to himself about his city habits. Once inside, Nina pulled her wet clothes away from herself and fanned them as if that would help them dry. They sat for a few minutes in silence watching the rain.

Jonathan drove slowly on the gravel roads. It was hard to see as the wind thrashed around them, the rain seeming to come from all directions at once. "It's like being inside a washing machine," Nina said as she peered out the front windshield. Neither of them spoke again until they'd reached Highway 34 and were headed into Lincoln.

"You up for a martini at the Tam?" he said.

"Sure am." He and Nina shared a mutual appreciation for out-of-the-way bars. Although there were better martinis to be had in Lincoln, none of the places that served them could compete with the ambiance of the Tam-O'Shanter. It had what Jonathan always referred to as the "vital sleaze factor."

He drove down o Street, noting the changes. It was a different city than the one he remembered from his childhood. He knew there were now film festivals and venues for new music. He'd even heard recently about a bar with one of those whiz kid bartenders mixing the sort of trendy drinks made on the spot that were all the rage in Boston's hipster bars.

He parked in front of the Tam, and they waited for a break in the rain before running inside. The dimness of the bar felt slightly unsettling to Jonathan. No matter how much time had passed, he always felt a momentary battle with the habits of his upbringing whenever he sought out a place of such self-indulgence.

Nina, who suffered no such neuroses, greeted the bartender, an older woman whose yellow hair was swept up in an elaborate beehive Jonathan guessed she'd worn her entire adult life. The bartender returned Nina's greeting without enthusiasm and gestured for them to sit anywhere they liked. They slid into one of the black leather booths, where Nina patted affectionately the red shag carpeting lining the wall next to the booth.

When she looked back at Jonathan, her expression shifted to concern. "You okay?"

Jonathan shrugged.

"Did something happen?"

"I'm all right. Just doing a lot of thinking today."

Nina nodded with understanding. Her father had died in her early twenties. Jonathan had never met him, and Nina rarely talked about him, though he knew she had regrets. She'd often mentioned her concern that he wasn't on good terms with his parents, suggesting at times that he might regret it someday. He guessed this was the someday she'd been referring to.

After their martinis came, Jonathan tipped his glass to Nina, his eyes intent on hers, and she met his glass with a similarly intense gaze. Nina and her sisters believed that if those toasting didn't look into one another's eyes, it would result in seven years without sex.

Nina set down her glass. "Would you mind if I tried Betsy to see how everything's going at the house?"

He nodded for her to go ahead and listened half-attentively as she went through her usual checklist accounting for each of the animals. Nina laughed at one point and took the phone away to relate to Jonathan. "The new kitty got into Lo's bed, and Lo went nuts." She laughed again, but Jonathan felt bad for poor old Lo. She was already outnumbered by the cats, and now this. Nina didn't seem to notice his disapproval.

Unselfconscious Nina. He wondered if she ever questioned herself. If so, he'd never seen it. How he needed her. He thought again as he often had about the irony of his family's refusal to accept her because she wasn't Mennonite. It kept them from seeing how much they all had in common. She'd spent her life helping children at risk. She'd protested every war and arms buildup since Vietnam; she'd created cooperatives to help people in need, raised money for community improvements. She represented the heart and soul of the same ideals they subscribed to, and yet, this apparently uncrossable divide. And over what? An abstraction? A creed? A doctrine? A tradition? A history? A few magic words? He felt his own futility in bringing about understanding. Frankly, he was tired of the fight. Today he felt his age in a new way. Most startling of all, he felt a new sort of vulnerability in knowing his father's protection was gone from the world.

While Nina continued to talk, he decided to make a call of his own. Monty picked up immediately. "I didn't think I'd be hearing from you for a few days," Monty said.

"How's everything there?"

"Fine. We got Murray straightened out."

"Anything I should know about?"

"Tom called," Monty said. "When you get back, we need to get right to work on the estimate for the Beyers' place."

"They still insisting on using that god-awful fixture in the entryway?"

"Afraid so."

Jonathan sighed. "Do you really need me there for that?"

"I'd rather you were involved," Monty said. "They specifically asked for you."

Jonathan paused. Suddenly his life in Boston seemed far away. Monty picked up on his reluctance. "Hey, man. I didn't mean to pressure you. You've got a lot going on right now. Just focus on what you need to do. Okay? I can handle Beyers. And fuck 'em if they don't want to deal with me."

That was the thing about Monty. He and Jonathan went way back. There was no one in the world who knew Jonathan like Monty did. They'd had more adventures together than Jonathan could possibly tell. Sometimes it was only a word, and they'd both be somewhere else. You'd only have to say, "House in the woods," and they'd be back in Michigan to a night they'd been out drinking and hooked up with some local guy, one of those squirrely types they usually tried to avoid. Jonathan hadn't thought about that night for a long time, how they'd ended up, the three of them, going together to a party, when about two in the morning the guy had told Jonathan and Monty they could crash at his uncle's house. Jonathan had been dubious about it, but no, the guy had said, his uncle was cool. Monty had been driving, and he'd thought it sounded fine.

They drove a hell of a way into the woods that night. This was in the Upper Peninsula. Talk about generalized weirdness; it was another world up there. By the time they'd finally pulled up to the house, porch falling off the front, trees growing so thick you could hardly see the place until you were right up on it, Jonathan was sure the kid had taken them on a goose chase and had started getting suspicious again. "What's this?" he'd said.

"It's my uncle's place. What's your problem, man?" He remembered the kid had a snide way about him that somehow made Jonathan feel like an idiot. As they walked to the house, Jonathan got the creeps again, but this time he didn't say anything. Monty looked back at him once but kept on going.

Inside there was nothing in the living room, except they saw by the moonlight coming through the bare windows a circle of rifles, their bayonets stuck in the floor. That was all there was. "Jesus," Jonathan had said when they got inside. Monty hadn't said anything, but he'd looked at Jonathan like he was about to leave his skin. Monty finally shrugged, and the kid found them three military-issue bedrolls. He'd clearly crashed there before.

They were all still asleep the next morning, the sun shining in through the windows, when they heard something rustling. Jonathan looked up and saw a naked girl walking through the room. She walked right past the rifles in the floor like it was nothing. She was young. Really young. Fourteen maybe, if that. Blonde, pale.

She didn't even look at them as she headed to the bathroom. Then an older guy came into the room. He was only wearing boxer shorts, but even half-naked like that, they could see he was a guy you didn't want to mess with. Career military, the kid had told them. No shit.

The old guy bristled when he first saw them there on the floor then relaxed after he saw the kid. He'd been smoking a joint and offered it to them. Monty and the kid each took a hit, but Jonathan didn't want any. He wasn't comfortable at all with that scene. The girl came back into the room. Still naked, she wasn't one bit shy or embarrassed. Just stood there and took a hit off the joint the old guy handed her. He nodded his head toward the girl. Jonathan didn't think he'd said anything, but they'd all known what he meant. They couldn't say he hadn't been generous, but they'd passed on his offer. They hadn't stayed long after that. Monty and Jonathan were ready to go, and they figured this was the right time to ditch the kid.

After Jonathan got off the phone with Monty, Nina tipped her glass to his again. She smiled, and he didn't think he'd ever felt so happy knowing she was part of his life, that he had a life to return to with her in Boston.

After the storm, while her sisters opened the house, Elsa put on her over boots and went out to the vegetable garden. She liked to weed after a rain, and she needed to be at some task. The garden gate was stiff as she pushed it open. Inside the green beans and the beet tops had been pushed flat to the ground. A few longer tendrils had been broken off by the force of the storm. She stooped to pick them up. She'd kept the rows clean, but bindweed had started to climb the fence, and crabgrass seemed to have taken root overnight along the edge of the plot.

She couldn't help but think about how sin was like the weeds in a garden, a lesson about the ways of the human heart. You could never be too vigilant. Sin was always waiting, and if it was allowed to take root, it choked out every good thing. This was what she was attempting to root out in Anna June.

"Hi," she heard from the fence and looked up to see Pastor Roth. He'd found a pair of Haven's old boots, clearly much too big for him. As if guessing her thoughts, he smiled and pointed to his feet. "I hope you don't mind."

Elsa shook her head and straightened her back, using her wrist to push away a stray hair that had crept out of from beneath her prayer veil. She lifted her muddy hands as if appealing for his help.

"May I?"

"Certainly."

He walked into the garden, his feet sliding up and down inside the boots. He laughed at himself, and once again the years rolled off his face. He began to work across from her.

"Do you still have a garden, Donald?"

"Oh yes. Grace keeps saying we don't need so much, but I can't seem to stop planting the same big garden each year the way I did when there were five hungry children to feed." He laughed softly before adding, "We give away a lot. Some of it Grace cans and freezes, but a lot goes over to the men's shelter down the way from us."

Elsa was quiet for a few seconds as she tugged at an especially deep-rooted tuft of crabgrass. "I suppose I'll need to cut back next year," she said, not meaning for her voice to catch as it did.

Either Pastor Roth didn't notice or was too polite to point it out. "Yes. Everything has changed now," he said. Elsa felt tears start again. When she reached into her apron pocket for a Kleenex, she was stopped by her muddy hands; instead, she raised a shoulder to wipe dry each eye. Pastor Roth continued to work silently behind her.

The sun tried to come out again, creating a peach glow around the edges of the still-dark clouds. Late afternoon was Elsa's favorite time of the day. She'd need to feed the chickens soon. If Haven were still here, if everything were normal, she'd be gathering a pan of green beans about now, picking cucumbers, perhaps a few beets or radishes, thinking about what to make for supper. Never again, she thought. And that same brimming over of tears. She sniffed softly and snuck a quick peek at Pastor Roth, who still seemed engrossed in his own thoughts, working quietly along the fence.

She was glad to have him here, an old friend. She was terribly alone in the world. The gathering of friends and family only underscored how alone she really was. They all had lives to go back to. If she wasn't vigilant, they'd be swooping in, packing away her things, closing the house, and moving her to some horrid place "for her own good." If she had to leave, she wanted to do it on her own terms.

Before they had finished their work, the sky to the east cleared, and the sun shone blank and white. Farther west, though, a monstrous thunderhead was forming. Even as Elsa watched, it pushed and writhed high into the stratosphere. Squared off like an anvil at one end, the cloud was massive and dense, white and beautiful even as it menaced the sky. Though Elsa had never seen a cloud like it before in real life, it seemed familiar to her, like the clouds she'd seen in paintings. She almost expected to see angels descending from it as they would have in those paintings. She imagined they would be the angels sent to take Haven to his rest.

When Pastor Roth turned and noticed the cloud, she expected him to say something along the whimsical lines she'd been thinking about it being the chariot of the Lord, but instead he said, "Goodness, someone's getting quite the weather over yonder," reminding Elsa what the cloud really meant. Yes, someone was getting quite the weather.

They were still in the garden when the folks from the regional office of the Mennonite Central Committee pulled into the yard. They'd driven all day from Indiana and would be staying the night with church members who had opened their homes for them. When Elsa recognized who had arrived, she and Pastor Roth looked at one another with panic, like guilty kids caught playing in the mud.

Pastor Roth suggested they try sneaking in through the back

door and making themselves more presentable, but wouldn't you know it, the whole carload, not sure which door to use, had gone to the back door and caught them there looking like two drowned prairie dogs. It took them a few seconds to recognize Elsa, looking the way she did. No point in pretending. Pastor Roth made a joke of it, and they all laughed as they hugged Elsa, telling her not to worry about her muddy things. Then they all grew sober.

"Brother Haven was our most reliable man on a mission." That was Brother Marty Stauffer, director of the Midwest Disaster Relief Committee. "I always knew if I called Haven, he'd be there to help." Elsa felt a lightheaded pride as she listened. Haven had been gone a lot in their marriage, serving in these ways, and she was glad his service had been recognized. "We didn't take it for granted, the sacrifice you were making, Sister Elsa," Marty Stauffer went on. "Your support for the work of the Central Committee is appreciated, and the Lord will reward you for it. Now, too soon, Brother Haven has been taken from us, gone to his reward. We'll miss his good spirit, but the Lord must have wanted his fellowship."

Marty Stauffer had such a formal way about him Elsa was tempted to match it somehow. She made an awkward little curtsy and immediately felt embarrassed by the gesture, especially looking the way she did in her muddy clothes. The others in the group — Marty's wife, Lillian; the assistant director, David Yoder; and his pretty wife, Julia — all hung back a little as Marty spoke, clearly not well acquainted with Haven.

Julia Yoder admitted as much as they finally moved to go inside. "I regret not having gotten to know your husband better, Mrs. Grebel. I'm so sorry for your loss." Such nice manners, Elsa thought. Why didn't Jeffry and Kathy's grown daughters — Susan and Laurie — have such nice ways? They were so sullen when it came down to it, so lumpish. She remembered how when they were younger Susan and Laurie had been so pretty, much prettier than Anna June, but as girls they'd always seemed to her like unbaked dough, something not quite finished about them. Elsa had assumed this quality would pass as they grew up, but it hadn't. They'd only gotten older.

By contrast, Anna June was like a colt, all long legs and jangly nerves. She couldn't be in a room without you noticing, and she was in the kitchen now as Elsa followed her guests inside. Elsa removed her overboots and apologized again for her appearance. While she was talking, she caught Anna June's eye. Anna June smiled, and Elsa almost smiled back. It was like that with Anna June. She stole smiles from a person. Elsa caught herself and narrowed her eyes at the girl, noting as she did so how it confused her. Good. Let her be confused. That was her natural condition, the place where she had fallen by giving in to worldly pride. That's all it was: pride.

"Please sit down and have a cup of coffee," Elsa said now to her guests. She looked at Pastor Roth, who, like her, had removed his overboots on the back porch. His trousers were muddy on the bottom and the cuffs of his shirt too. "Donald, I'll find you something of Haven's to wear." He nodded and followed her.

Pastor Roth waited in the upstairs hallway as Elsa pulled out a shirt and a pair of pants from the closet. Haven had been a much larger man than Pastor Roth. "If you wear this belt with the pants, and if you cuff the legs and the sleeves of the shirt —"

"Don't you worry about me now, Elsa," Pastor Roth interrupted her.

"I'll just get your things into the wash quick," she added.

"You stop your fussing. I'll be fine. I'll find someone else to help me. Go back on down to your visitors."

Anna June went home and stayed there all afternoon. She even ate supper at home because she didn't feel comfortable anymore at Grandma's house. Daddy was watching television. He had his computer on at the same time, and he was excited because the radar was showing bad weather in York and Seward counties. He was always excited about bad weather. She saw a big yellow thing with a red center in it moving around on the map. She knew this meant a big storm. "See here, Squirt. See what's happening, just west of Seward there?" Daddy said. "I'll bet they're really getting hammered over toward York."

"Do you think Mr. Slocum's house will get the storm?"

"I wouldn't be surprised."

"This was a good year for crops, wasn't it?

"They're set for a bumper crop, and corn is at a record high this year too."

"I feel bad for the people who are getting hammered," Anna June said, and when she said it, she couldn't help but see hammers falling from the sky with the rain, even though she knew it was silly.

"That's life in Nebraska," Daddy said. "You can just count

on it. If this had been a more hospitable place, the early settlers would have stayed, but only the most stubborn and pathetic stayed on. That's our legacy, Sweet Pea."

Anna June didn't like when he said things like that. "The sign says, 'It's the Good Life.'"

Daddy laughed so hard at that he made a snorting sound. "Go tell those poor fools over in the next county this is the good life. See what they'll say to that today." After that Anna June decided not to say anything else to him. He'd just make fun. She called Celia on the phone, but Celia wasn't home. She knew she wasn't at the swimming pool because of the storm. She wanted to go over and hold Fritz for a while. More than ever she wished she had a dog. If she had a dog now, she could curl up on her bed and forget about everything with Grandma. She laid on her bed and looked at the ceiling. There was a water stain from when the roof had leaked. She hated that stain. Celia's dad would have fixed it for sure.

One of the cards in the secret history was the story of a boy named Billy Yantzen. Her dad had known him in school. "He wasn't right." That's what her dad had said. "Something wasn't right with him." When he was fourteen, Billy Yantzen hung himself in the basement of his house. Anna June thought about what that would feel like. Terrible, she guessed. Daddy had said he understood that boy sometimes, and Anna June hadn't liked him saying that. She felt like she needed to keep an eye on Daddy some days for fear of what he could do. Right now was one of those times. Even feeling as bad as she did about Grandma not liking her anymore, Anna June couldn't see hanging herself. She could almost imagine how it would feel, and it made her sick thinking about it.

The sun was out again by the time Jonathan and Nina started back to the farm. In spite of the changes, Lincoln seemed like a small town to him. When he was a kid, going into Lincoln meant going to the big city. He remembered going to the basketball tournament the year Jeffrey was on the team and they'd made it to the state championship. It had been a big deal, his being on that team, such a big deal that even their mother had gone to watch the tournament.

One of Jonathan's most vivid memories of his brother Daniel was the two of them playing together under the bleachers of Pershing Auditorium and their excitement when their father bought them hotdogs. He remembered then how Daniel had scavenged for treasures amid the trash beneath the bleachers, filling his empty drink cup with pennies and bits of plastic and other odds and ends. He would have been only four or five at the time.

It was on a particularly bad stretch off Highway 6, where the gravel had been washed away by the storm and the car kept slipping on the muddy roadbed, that Nina told him about how she wanted to take Anna June back with them to Boston. Jonathan wrestled with the steering wheel as she laid out the details of the plan she and his mother had devised. She seemed entirely unaware of the family dynamics, unaware that his mother was practicing her own version of the old Mennonite habit of shunning. It would have broken his father's heart to see the way his mother had turned against his beloved Anna June.

Jonathan knew in part he was invoking his father's wishes in order to protect himself. He'd need all the ammunition he could get to overcome the combined energies of his mother and Nina. Until he could develop a strategy, though, he chose to keep his mouth shut. Hell, what choice did he have against Nina's enthusiasm and his mother's stubbornness?

While he thought about this, Jonathan found himself driving too fast on the soft road. The car fishtailed, and he felt a surge of adrenaline as he fought against the wheel; he imagined for a split second he might lose control, imagined going into the ditch, the car flipping over with them inside. His heart raced even after he'd righted the vehicle and slowed down.

Oblivious, beside him Nina continued to talk. In her mind all the details were complete. She'd get Anna June into art classes. They'd apply immediately to the Commonwealth School. "It's the perfect school for a girl like Anna June," she said. "And while we're establishing residency, we can supplement her education at home." What could go wrong? Nina, as usual, had jumped in with both feet. He knew from past arguments how much she resented being reminded of times when a little forethought might have avoided a lot of trouble.

Once they arrived at the house, he glanced quickly into the workshop. He had cleaned up his mess, but he still felt chastened at the memory of his tantrum earlier in the day.

A steady crowd had been coming and going, and in their absence new folks had arrived. At first Jonathan hadn't recognized the women from the big trip to DC as he and Nina entered the

126

house that afternoon; instead, he'd mistaken their granddaughters for them. The family resemblances were powerful, and time had played a trick on him. Truth was, they hadn't been all that much older than he'd been back then; they'd only seemed older — all of them married with kids, matronly already in their early twenties.

He had to admit to himself that despite their willful dowdiness, he still found young Mennonite women incredibly sexy. It wasn't a taste he thought he could explain to his friends in Boston. There was something, though, about their modesty, their deference, their very plainness, that thrilled him as he guessed what might lie beneath that protective exterior. After all, a naked woman with her hair down was still a naked woman. He could imagine in the democracy of the bedroom these young women could rival any woman who had devoted herself to cultivating beauty. The difference was how quickly they acquiesced to age, how quickly they moved past that stage of sexual attractiveness — both men and women — to take up their roles as adults, parents, church workers, and community members. He doubted he'd ever be able to explain this to anyone else either, but he found all of them more confident and more centered than he did many of his more sophisticated friends. When he thought about grown-ups, he always thought about the Mennonite brethren.

Once he'd recognized them, the women made a fuss over him just as they'd done when he was a kid, making him feel like he was seventeen again instead of fifty-eight. He'd been the only male in the group from their church going to DC to protest the war. They'd traveled together in an old school bus that summer. He'd been surrounded by those teasing, sunny women and their serious mission, with their sack lunches, sleeping along the way on the floors of church basements, singing together on the long drive. It was perhaps the happiest time of his life.

And then he'd seen Karalee in the sun at a kiosk on the National Mall, buying popcorn and locking her blue eyes with his—nothing simple in those eyes—his knees almost buckling, every nerve in his body at attention, suddenly in service to only one thing, remaining in her presence. He'd followed her, pushing against people, desperate to keep her in his sight, watching as she joined a group, and finally standing dumbstruck before her until she'd laughed and held out her popcorn for him to share in the same way one might address a silly child or a fool. He'd been both.

Later she told him she'd thought he was handsome, that she'd thought his look was contrived, his "thing" to look like a hick. Everything was "cool" then. Whatever your "bag." That was how she had talked. Only later, when she saw him with the Mennonite ladies, did she realize it wasn't an act; he was the real deal, a real hick, but from one of the peace churches, which was authentic, and "she could dig that." She'd shared with him a tab of acid, and they'd lain together on the grass, and the world had been revealed to him, every seam, every system, so that he saw it all and understood it, despite never again being able to articulate it or see it in such sharp focus; it had changed his life forever. Nothing was like he'd been taught. And once he'd become aware like that, he couldn't pretend not to know.

The church ladies had teased him on the ride home about how quiet he was, trying, he could see, to cheer him up, for they'd seen him with the "English" girl with the red hair and the shockingly short miniskirt. They thought his sulkiness was nothing more than youthful longing. They didn't yet see how his silence all the way home was the prelude to a more final revolt.

The church folks later gave the ladies who'd been on the trip with him a hard time. "What'd you do to Jonathan?" At first Jonathan hadn't let anyone know he'd continued his relationship with the girl he'd met, the Wisconsin farm girl turned u of Wisconsin campus radical, Karalee Taylor, who he'd been writing to regularly since returning from the trip. He had fuel to keep alive his interest, for her letters arrived every other day at half the pace his were sent to her.

Senior year his grades plummeted, and his sullen disregard for home and church challenged his mother's commitment to silence over the matter, her only weapon, after all, and what he most wanted from her at that time. His father could speak, and did speak, volumes in one word, Son, a word so nuanced as to question, console, and correct all at once. And yet Jonathan had persisted, as had Karalee. Their love had seemed real to them. No one could have told them differently, and to this day, if he'd been inclined to speak so melodramatically, he'd still say she'd been the love of his life.

They'd lived together, and they'd loved one another, and they'd had a boy named Timothy. It should have been his life. "She's English," his mother had said. "You know we can't mingle with English; you know we can't be unequally yoked." But he had mingled. He had meant to mingle his whole life with hers, except he'd underestimated the power of refusal, the corrosive power of silence, how long his mother could outlast him, how quickly she would capitalize on their first rocky patch, how vulnerable he would be to his own hurt, how Timothy would become the pawn, the child who needed to be rescued from the unsaved. There'd been no excuse for his not realizing his mother's capacity for refusal. He'd been a witness to it his entire life.

That was a long time ago. None of them even knew where Karalee was anymore. And Tim, queer as a three-dollar bill — not that it mattered, of course — coming yesterday, saying the Jesus word, and his grandmother, like a trained chicken, automatically giving him whatever he wanted: forgiveness, a handout, a free pass. Jeffrey knew the secret password too. How easy to placate her. "Jesus loves me." That's all it took. She'd take care of the rest, endlessly indulge any aberrant behavior. She wanted to hear what she wanted to hear. There was no reality other than that conceived by his mother, and woe be to the person who in any way contradicted her version of things.

Once she got settled back downstairs that afternoon, Marty Stauffer presented Elsa with a bundle of sympathy cards from the conference offices. "There'll be more coming, Sister Elsa," he said. "These are just from the Midwest offices. Everyone who knew Haven loved him."

As he spoke, Elsa felt an unexpected pinch of resentment. She'd almost forgotten it after all these years, but there it was again, an old enemy skulking along the back wall of her mind. She recognized it immediately from her years as a young woman, a young mother, burdened with the farm and the boys and Haven answering every call that came from the MCC. And what could she say to that? Earthquakes. Tornadoes. Floods. Fires. Wars. So much suffering: people hungry, cold, frightened, homeless. People shattered by disaster. Their need had always been greater than hers, no matter what. How could she dare complain? And she hadn't. Except in her heart. She'd sometimes seethed for days after Haven had left, feeling sharply his absence. He'd always hired one of the girls from the church to help her, but what she'd wanted was him, not help. She'd felt so small and so alone with those mean thoughts of hers. She'd prayed many days for deliverance and forgiveness, but still, always, the sneaking lowness of her resentment. And here it was again, still with her after all this time, when she thought she'd been delivered.

The worst had been in the spring the year Jeffrey was sixteen — that terrible year — when Haven left for two weeks. She'd begged him not to go, and his answer had been to bring her sister Eleanor to stay while he was away. There had been a long time after that when she wasn't sure she could forgive him, both for leaving and for humiliating her in front of her sister that way. She didn't know how she'd gotten through it. Everything had taken such effort; she'd felt as if her feet were stuck in concrete and her head full of mattress stuffing.

After supper Anna June thought about the promise she'd made to sleep in Grandma's room. She didn't want to go back to Grandma's house, but she had to. She snuck through the back door and upstairs, where she saw Timothy's sleeping bag on the floor. She didn't want to be in the same room with him, but they'd made a promise, and they needed to keep their promise.

She decided she'd wait outside in the barn until after bedtime. Before she could leave the house, Nina saw her and smiled. Anna June was glad somebody still liked her, even if it was only Nina.

Nina asked Anna June how she was doing.

"Not so good."

"It's been a long, sad day, hasn't it?"

"Grandma's mad at me."

Nina asked if she wanted to talk about it, and Anna June shook her head no, wishing she hadn't said anything to Nina about it.

"Do you feel like sitting on the porch awhile?" Nina said. Anna June followed Nina onto the porch, hoping Grandma wouldn't see her.

The sun was starting to set, and someone turned on the lights in the house. Inside it was noisy with so many people talking.

Uncle Jonathan's friends had come out, and they were playing basketball by the workshop. The cicada droned, and the fireflies winked in the grass and trees.

"It's a nice evening, isn't it?" Nina said. "Nebraska is someplace I'd never have seen if I hadn't married your uncle." Anna June didn't say anything to that. "Have you ever been to the ocean, Anna June?"

"No."

"I grew up near the ocean, so I'm partial to it. I think it's the most beautiful place in the world," Nina said. "When I was a girl, we went every summer to the Cape for a month." She looked at Anna June. "Cape Cod's a place on the sea. When we were at the Cape as kids, we spent all day every day in our swimsuits. At night all the kids built fires on the beach. It was a wonderful place to be in the summer." She smiled at Anna June. "Would you ever want to come visit Jonathan and me in Boston? We could take you to our house on the Cape."

Anna June thought about it for a few seconds. "I suppose that would be all right. How would I get there?"

"You'd have to fly. Have you ever been on an airplane?"

"Nope."

"You'd get the hang of it. Maybe we could plan something for later this summer."

Anna June felt better having someone to talk to, so she listened, and she sort of started to like Nina a little more.

"Can you talk to your parents about what's happening with your grandmother?" Nina asked.

"No way. They wouldn't be able to help." Anna June looked quickly at Nina to see how she would take this, but Nina only nodded.

"Sometimes that's how it is with parents," she said, and Anna June waited. She guessed Nina might keep talking, and she did. "When I was a kid, I loved my father, but he was gone all the time, and I was always mad at him about that. I thought he didn't love us."

Anna June wondered why he was gone all the time, and Nina told her he had a demanding job as the head of the marketing department for a pharmaceutical company.

Anna June didn't know what that was, but she didn't say anything. Nina said, "I started to understand him better when I got older. You'll probably understand your parents better when you're older too."

Anna June didn't think that would ever happen. "What did you understand?" she asked.

Nina looked out at the sky for a few seconds before she answered. "My father was very sad. He was unhappy with his life, and yet he kept doing the same things year after year, going to a job he didn't like and commuting for hours every day, and well . . ." Nina was quiet for a while before she said, "He used to write us girls a letter every Christmas. He'd stay up late after we'd gone to bed on Christmas Eve, and he'd write these long letters from Santa. At our house we didn't leave milk and cookies for Santa; we left a bottle of red wine and a pack of Camels." She laughed and shook her head. Anna June looked up quickly. Wine and cigarettes! Two terrible sins.

Nina didn't seem to think anything about it. She said, "We'd get up on Christmas morning, and we'd find these six-page letters complaining about the terrible year Santa'd had: trouble with the elves, rebellions among the reindeer, horrid weather, the rigors of having to plan for Christmas Day, and the long, long trip on Christmas Eve to bring everyone their presents and the complaints of everyone who didn't like what they got. They were the strangest letters, always stained with red wine and smudged where he'd erased. The ashtray on the kitchen table would be full of cigarette butts. We kept all those letters, and after he died, my sisters and I read them again. We laughed ourselves silly. They were so funny. And at the same time, they were so sad, because they were Dad's way of saying how he felt about his life at the time." Nina looked at Anna June. "Do you know that feeling of laughing and crying at the same time?"

Did she ever. All day she'd been feeling that exact way.

Nina told her a lot of things about the ocean and about Boston and about how she met Uncle Jonathan. She told Anna June about how on her first date with Jonathan she was trying to impress him and how she flubbed up. "We were eating lunch, and I was trying to act cool," she said. "I lowered my head without looking at my drink, but instead of finding the straw with my mouth, it went up my nose. I figured if I just lifted my head casually, the straw would come out and Jonathan would never notice anything, but wouldn't you know that stupid straw stayed stuck, so there I was looking at Jonathan with a straw hanging out of my nose." Anna June couldn't help but laugh with Nina. "Jonathan always says that's when he fell in love with me. He still teases me sometimes about it, asking me when we order drinks if I'd like a straw for my nose."

Anna June laughed again. They were quiet for a while before Nina said, "I should probably go back inside and help. I'll see you in the morning, Anna June. I know it's going to be a hard day for you tomorrow night with the viewing and all. If you need to get away or need someone to talk to, you can always talk to me."

Jonathan's old friends — all of them still practicing Mennonites — had grown rounder and ruddier with age, so that at first he hadn't recognized them. Finally, he remembered each one because of a smile, a manner of speech, a familiar gesture: Mike, Jim, Merle, Clyde, and Dwain. He hadn't seen them in years, but they were as friendly and open-faced as they'd always been. Beneath the suit of age, Jonathan saw, they were still the boys he'd hunted frogs with and walked beans and detasseled corn with. They'd memorized Bible verses together, tried smoking cigarettes, teased each other about girls, and learned to drive in cow pastures together. All of them were still living in the area, continuing the lives they'd been destined to live.

They weren't the sort of men to sit around the house, and Jonathan wasn't surprised when after they'd paid the necessary toll of a piece of pie and coffee, Mike suggested they shoot a few hoops. At the suggestion Jonathan was out the door and halfway through inflating the basketball he'd remembered seeing under his father's workbench earlier that day by the time the guys joined him.

"Three on three," Clyde said. He'd been the best player of

the bunch in high school. Although Jonathan appeared to be the most fit of the group, he was surprised by how strong and agile his old friends were. He fought for every point he made and had to work to guard them, especially Dwain, who had always been wicked quick. Jonathan laughed a few times as Dwain faked him out and got under the hoop.

They'd known each other since way back, but Jonathan sensed their silent confusion over his life's choices. He knew all of them well enough to know they weren't as uncomplicated as they appeared. Tonight under the twilight sky he felt there was something admirable about them, something deeply authentic about their lives, something real. They were happy. He could see that. These were contented men.

When the game began, the sun was starting to set. Now, as the game came to an end, a full moon rose amid the busy glow of fireflies.

It was only then they all grew awkward with Jonathan. Merle finally broke the silence, hugging Jonathan roughly. "Sure am sorry about your Dad, buddy." The others followed Merle's lead with variations on that theme. "Your dad was a good man." "See you at the funeral, Jon." "Take care of yourself." And then Clyde, "You're in the Lord's hands, brother," and the awkwardness again as everyone felt the inappropriateness of addressing Jonathan as a fellow believer, when he was so clearly among the fallen away.

Jonathan watched as the guys all got into their Fords and Chevy's and Buicks, switched on their headlights at the same time so that he was blinded for a few seconds, and one by one turned their vehicles around and filed out of the driveway onto the gravel road. After they left, the more subtle night sounds — crickets, bullfrogs, and screech owls — that had been masked by the noise of their game returned, and it suddenly seemed late. On the night air Jonathan smelled an earthy vegetable brew, a smell unique to summer nights in eastern Nebraska: corn in full tassel, new-mown grass, damp earth, a slight and not unpleasant smell of cow manure from neighboring farms. He breathed in, drawing the smells deep into his lungs, wanting suddenly to store it in his cells so he could call it forth later when he was far from home. What an odd thought. He hadn't thought of this farm as home for decades. He'd wanted nothing so much as to be far away from this place, and yet here he was tonight wanting to take it with him in some way.

When he got into their room later, Nina couldn't quit talking to him about Anna June. "I'm completely blown away by that kid," she said, and Jonathan felt a twinge of irritation. Something about her perception of Anna June as a talented, eccentric little girl stranded (according to Nina) in a place that couldn't understand her talent appealed to Nina's deepest impulse to rescue.

"Now that your dad's gone," Nina said, "who's going to support her? At least they had one another." Nina got a wistful look on her face, an expression he called her "pre-adoption look."

"Nina," he said, his voice cautioning.

"I know." She barely took a breath, though, before adding, "But really, Jonathan. She would thrive in a creative and disciplined environment —"

"Nina," he said again. "It isn't our place."

"Whose place is it if not ours?" Nina said. She'd never been one for knowing her place. "Honestly, Jonathan, I can't leave her here. It just isn't right. She needs more direction than she's ever going to get here. Maybe if your family lived in Lincoln or Omaha . . . maybe if they were the type to seek out opportunities, but you know as well as I do, they aren't." Jonathan knew well how Nina could get an idea into her head and not let go. He knew well how she could push and without really meaning to become a bully. There was a streak of self- righteousness in her that she couldn't see herself, and he'd never had much luck reasoning with her when she was in what he called her "do-gooder mode."

"I know, sweetie," he finally said. "I do know. Let's talk about it later, though. Right now I'm going back outside for a while. Okay? Don't wait up for me."

The day before, Tim had given him an envelope first thing after he'd arrived. "A present for you, Pop," he'd said. "Something to help you get through." Inside had been two joints. The barn was quiet, and Jonathan climbed up to the haymow. He stuck his legs out the haymow door like he had when he was a kid, took two hits off a joint, and lay back, resting his head on his arms. It was good stuff, powerful, the way pot was these days so that he was immediately stoned. For the first time ever, though, he felt not so much high as tired — old and worn-out. He supposed it was the way he'd been thinking about the past all day, thinking about his father and Karalee. What had happened with her and his family had happened forty years ago. He'd lived an entire life since then. And yet there was something unresolved at the core of it. Until today he hadn't seen it that way.

He took another hit off the joint. Instead of relaxing him, it made him feel jittery. He was a man who kept himself busy. He kept fit; he kept informed; he kept on task. He didn't like to have idle time. He thought tonight how he was known in the lighting design industry for his innovations, using what others considered castaways to create unique effects and unusual fixtures. He was always thinking, always creating. He wasn't a designer in the sense of working regularly with wholesalers. He was someone who just as often sought out estate sales and thrift stores, bought odd lots on eBay, and although he had a fancy downtown office, what he really did was extend the life of things, find new uses for what had been discarded. As he thought about his work tonight, he had an uncomfortable chain of thought. He sat up and hugged his knees against his chest.

In graduate school he'd studied theorists of design and had found few of them quite to his liking. His thesis, which he had until this moment somehow believed was original — mainly because his advisor had felt it was and had helped him publish it so that others had agreed with its originality — he saw now was completely derivative. He hadn't seen the need to acknowledge the influence of this farm. He'd exploited his own inheritance and had actually believed himself a trailblazer.

Throughout the day, without quite realizing it, he'd been looking around the farm, really looking, as one does at last things. The aesthetic of the outbuildings in particular, he saw, were examples of his proclivities for the use of stripped-down industrial materials — galvanized metal, brooder lights, barn lights, the utilitarian products ubiquitous throughout rural America. On previous visits to Nebraska he'd scoured auctions and farm sales for raw materials; he'd ordered in bulk from suppliers like Wheelers and Farm Supply, arguably the only lighting designer in Boston to have such vendors. He'd been mimicking for years the effect of the light in this barn, and still he hadn't thought to credit his past.

Nina must have seen it. She surely noticed it the first time she'd visited the farm. In memory he saw her again, walking slowly around the house and the farmyard, carefully taking note of the hardware and the fixtures. She wouldn't have missed anything, least of all the provenance for his own taste, and yet she had never breathed a word to suggest the connection, probably knowing what his reaction would be. Or was it more complicated? Was she uncomfortable with the realization that what she'd at first believed was his "amazing originality" was simply what he'd grown up with?

Despite Nina's loyalty, tonight Jonathan wanted more than anyone else in the world to talk to Karalee. He tried to imagine what she might say in this situation. One thing was for sure, she'd shake things up. Fuck this nicey nice. That would never do, and she wouldn't care whom she offended, including his mother. Dishonesty offended Karalee mightily.

Why was he thinking of Karalee in the past tense, he wondered, when he was sure she was alive somewhere in the world? Tim had last heard from her seven years earlier, when she was living in St. Thomas, shacked up — Tim's word — with an Australian who managed a resort down there. No doubt, she'd since moved on. Jonathan never worried about Karalee. She had an uncanny ability to land on her own two feet, and she had a way of getting what she wanted that went beyond her sexuality, so even if she'd let herself go — which seemed entirely possible — she'd still be a force to be reckoned with.

Knowing her as he had, Jonathan wasn't sure why he'd been so surprised by the affair with his friend Lyle. After all, they'd both had affairs during their marriage. But this time had been different. There'd been something angry and hurtful about it, something mean-spirited. She'd been sending a message. Whatever it was, he'd left without listening, and now in memory he could see Karalee's face, her surprise at the suddenness of his changing the rules, reverting to church guy, the hypocrite on his high horse, about her behavior. She may even have shouted something to this effect after him. And had he actually called her a slut? Could that be possible? Even then, she must have expected it all to blow over, like all of their fights eventually had. What she hadn't planned on was Elsa. He'd gone home, and he'd taken Tim with him. The custody battle had come as a shock to her.

Later, not long before she finally gave up trying to work it out with him and his parents to see Tim, Karalee had called him one night. He'd heard the resignation in her voice. She hadn't been angry or tearful; she'd been pulled together. "This is beneath you, Jonathan," she'd said, "letting your mother loose like this, using her to punish me. The only one who'll get hurt in this sordid little story will be Tim." And only as she'd said Tim's name had Jonathan heard a muffled sob. She'd been a good mother, and Jonathan had loved her still, more than ever at that moment. He'd wanted to go back and make it work with her. What had stopped him? Why hadn't he gone back?

He and Karalee had been thoughtful, surprisingly thoughtful, about having a baby in the first place, waiting several years before getting pregnant. She'd given birth at home with a midwife. After Tim was born, they'd done yoga with him and fed him only wholesome food, none of that canned crap for their baby, all cotton clothing. They hadn't been careless people, and yet they'd somehow let their life together slip away from them.

Here he was, almost sixty years old, stoned and sitting in the half-light of a barn he felt was the only church he knew, and he could finally see his father for who he was — an old man who'd never intended any harm. His entire life had been devoted to the best of intentions, and Jonathan had been in a pissing match with that old man for forty years; he was still in one with his frail, elderly mother. He could see how wrongheaded it all was and could see just as clearly how nothing would change. As soon as his mother opened her mouth again, he'd be right back where he'd been with her his entire adult life.

It was starting over again with her too, what with her shunning Anna June the way she was. Jonathan hadn't thought Anna June had it in her to stand up to his mother the way she had. Thinking about it, he felt himself smile in the dark. Crazy kid. He'd expected her to buckle under the pressure. She was just like Jeffrey in that way, not arguing or throwing a tantrum, simply refusing, and being better at refusing than the chief refuser herself, Elsa Grebel. He'd never been able to hold his own with his mother. It's why he'd had to go so far away.

For a while, before he'd moved to Boston, he'd lived at World's End in Hingham. That's where he'd wanted to be at that point in his life, as far from the farm and his parents as he could get. Before that he'd been on Kodiak Island. One foot in the country, one foot out, slowly edging back after years away. For years he'd found every expatriate community he could in Europe and Asia, staying for a while before moving on. He'd been running from his life with Karalee, never able to get far enough away to forget her, until he'd finally landed in more trouble than he could have imagined possible.

Jonathan had thought he was alone in the barn when he heard a sniffle in the darkness below. He came to full attention as he listened. Another sniffle. Whoever it was didn't seem to know he was there. He stood up quietly, hoping to leave without being noticed.

"Who is it?" Anna June's voice stopped him as he started down the haymow ladder. He waited until he'd finished his descent. "It's Jonathan."

"Oh," Anna June said. He heard the tears in her voice and, against his better judgment, moved in her direction. He found her near the old holding pens. In the semidarkness he could see her head was resting on her upraised knees. She didn't look up at him even as he slid down next to her. "Don't be nice to me," she said.

"Okay."

"Everything's going wrong."

"I heard that."

"If you're here to try to talk me out of it, you can go away."

"I'm not here for any reason. I just don't want to go back into the house."

Anna June still didn't look up, but Jonathan sensed she was listening. They sat like this for several minutes. Finally, Anna June raised her head and wiped her eyes with both palms. "Grandma's so mad at me."

"I know."

"I've never seen her mad like this before. She won't talk to me. She won't even look at me."

"I know."

"Daddy says that's her way, but she's never done it to me before."

Jonathan was quiet for a moment. "Well, Anna June," he said finally. "I'm not sure what happened, but until now you've always done exactly what she wanted."

"I just made some cards with stories my dad told me about the church, and I found stories in old newspapers like Grandma showed me. I want to keep the cards. I worked on them. I like the real stories best." Jonathan didn't say anything to this, and Anna June continued. "Even if I tore up the cards like Grandma wants, I'd still have the stories in my mind."

"That's what she's afraid of."

They sat for a long time in silence. They may have both dozed. Through the open barn door Jonathan watched now as moths circled the farm light in the driveway. The rain earlier that day had brought out the mosquitoes, and bats swooped in and out of the light in pursuit.

"How about we go for a drive?" he said, surprising himself with the suddenness of the idea.

"Okay," Anna June said, sounding a little dubious.

"Let's meet at Grandpa's truck in fifteen minutes."

Anna June shrugged. He wasn't sure from her response if she'd actually agreed to meet him or had just mollified him so he'd leave her alone. She was a squirrely kid, and why wouldn't she be?

The night had started with a clear sky, but as it had grown more humid, the thick air softened the edges of everything. As Jonathan walked back to the house, he felt as he often did on gray days in Boston, in a meditative twilight state, someplace between waking and dreaming.When he saw his mother crouching by the fence of the chicken yard, he thought maybe he was imagining her there. But no. It was really her. She didn't notice him as she baby-talked her rooster through the fence.

Sensing a presence then, she stood up. "You scared me, Jonny."

"I'm sorry."

"Your friends all go home?"

"Yes."

"That was nice of them to come out."

He agreed that it was and paused before saying, "I wonder if we could talk, Mother."

"Isn't that what we're doing?"

"You know what I mean."

"I'm afraid I don't."

He felt himself grow impatient with her and willed himself to remain civil as he asked why she was making it so difficult.

"What are you trying to say, Jonathan?"

"I'm trying to say, Mother . . . this thing with Anna June. Please don't do it. Don't let it get started."

"Why are you making this my fault, Jonathan?"

"I'm not trying to blame you, Mother. It's just —"

"I wish your father were here," she interrupted. "He'd know how to set things to right. He'd know how to talk to her. Anna June would never have stood up to him like she has me."

She was probably right about that. His father had a way of gently and quietly making you feel like absolute shit. No doubt, Anna June wouldn't have been invulnerable to the Haven Grebel effect. Jeffrey would be no help. He'd in fact probably rather goad Anna June on than discourage her.

"You'd think," his mother went on, "a kid does something destructive and then disrespects her elders . . . you'd think everyone would understand why —"

"Why what?"

"Why I can't countenance it."

"You don't have to countenance it, Mother." Jonathan wanted to add, "Don't get into a pissing match with a kid," but he stopped himself and said instead, "She's a kid, Mother. She's just a kid. Why can't you let it roll off you, wait it out?"

He felt his mother bristle. Just what he'd feared. It was laughable really, him giving advice. He knew not to say another word. He'd been an idiot to try. "I'm sorry to have interrupted you," he said, remembering as he turned to go that he was apologizing for interrupting her conversation with a rooster.

The house was still ablaze, every window lit up. In the kitchen a few of the neighbor women were straightening things. The living room was still crowded with people. They were singing together, his niece Susan at the piano and Pastor Roth on the harmonica.

Softly and tenderly, Jesus is calling,
Calling for you and for me;
See, on the portals He's waiting and watching,
Watching for you and for me.

Come home . . . come home.
Ye who are weary, come home.

147

Anna June liked the barn but not so much at night. It was dark, and she felt scared. She felt so scared she started to cry. It was partly because she missed Grandpa and partly because she felt bad about Grandma being mad at her. Everything was going wrong. This had been a bad day. The worst day ever. The moon was red when it first peeked over the horizon. Anna June thought it looked like it was trying to see if it was safe to come out. If it had asked her, she would have said no, it isn't safe. Stay where you are. But when the moon started to get higher in the sky, she was glad for it. It made the barn feel less scary to her.

Anna June must have gone to sleep for a while because when she woke up it was very late at night. She still didn't want to go into the house. She could hear people inside singing, and she didn't want to see Grandma. That's when she heard someone coming down the ladder of the haymow. It scared her about to death until Uncle Jonathan said it was him, and he found her over by the holding pens.

He sat down beside her, sliding down the wall like a kid would. "Don't be nice to me," Anna June said.

They were both quiet for a long time. Maybe they both slept

a little. Their heads were resting on their knees. Finally, Uncle Jonathan had asked if she wanted to go for a drive in the truck. Anna June had said yes, but now that they were walking toward the truck, she told him, "I don't know how to drive. I mean, I could probably figure it out, but I've never driven the truck."

Uncle Jonathan smiled. "That's okay. I know how." Anna June was surprised he knew how to drive a truck. He was wearing his everyday clothes, but they still looked fancy to her. They got into the pickup, and when she saw Grandpa's work gloves, she picked them up and started to sniff them, before she remembered Uncle Jonathan was there. He saw her. "You miss him a lot," he said.

Anna June watched as Uncle Jonathan put in the clutch, turned the key, and knew just how to jiggle it to get the truck started. "It goes into reverse hard," she said, but Uncle Jonathan got it into reverse without it hanging up.

"Let's go to the pond," he said.

The moon was full. It, and the lights from the truck, lit up the pasture in front of them. The truck rattled as they drove over the rough grass.

"I think it might be good for you to see where the accident happened," Uncle Jonathan said, and Anna June couldn't say no. Ever since starting the truck, he'd started looking different to her. Even with his fancy clothes, she could see he'd driven a truck before. He seemed comfortable driving in the pasture at night. And she could see he was one of them. Underneath everything he was one of them.

When they reached the pond, Uncle Jonathan parked the truck across from the hedge of angels. Before he turned off the headlights, it looked like the angels were standing on a stage with lights. They looked even more alive at night. She'd never seen them like that before. Uncle Jonathan nodded toward them. "Your soldiers are impressive."

"They aren't soldiers."

"Oh?"

"They're angels. To protect the water."

Uncle Jonathan looked confused. "The pond?"

"The water underneath the ground. The aquifer."

He smiled and nodded. "I know who's been talking to you."

"They're a hedge. It's from the Bible, from Ezekiel. God needed someone to stand in the gap, so I made the angels. They're God's soldiers, the angels, to protect the land . . . the water under the land."

"I see," Uncle Jonathan said, but Anna June didn't think he saw. She didn't try to explain any more.

"Let's get out," he said. The night was hazy, and the moon was huge. She saw the moon's reflection on the water of the pond. It made a foggy path of light on the water. Uncle Jonathan had been wearing glasses while he was driving, but now he took them off. Anna June followed him down to the pond. She watched as he stepped into the mud and slime at the edge of the water with his nice shoes. He didn't pay any mind to them. He looked back at her where she'd stopped on the pasture grass.

"This is where it happened," he said, but he wouldn't have needed to tell her that. Anna June could see the tracks made by the tractor and the ones made by the loader they'd used to pull it out of the water. The grass on the edge was all torn up from it. She hated how it looked.

Neither of them said anything for a long time. Something rustled in the grass nearby, and then it was quiet. Only the sound of the bullfrogs and the water making a kissing sound where it met the shore.

"I always loved this place," Uncle Jonathan said. Anna June didn't know if he meant the pond or the farm, and she didn't ask. Finally, he said, "There's a car in this pond."

"Really?" That got her curiosity. She walked closer to the edge and looked in.

"You can't see it."

"What kind of car?"

"A yellow Pontiac. It belonged to your Grandpa. First and only new car he ever owned."

"Did he drive it into the pond?"

"He put it in the pond."

"Grandpa did that? Why?"

"That car . . . well, it grieved your grandma to see it." Anna June didn't say anything. She knew he'd keep talking. "Your dad had been driving the Pontiac." Uncle Jonathan was quiet for a long time, but finally he said, "He was sixteen. He was only sixteen." Uncle Jonathan said it like he was talking to himself. When he got quiet this time, Anna June heard a loud banging. She heard a screeching like big birds. She heard a sound like cows bellowing after they're separated from their calves. "Our little brother . . ." Uncle Jonathan said. He didn't finish. Instead, he put his head down and pinched the top of his nose. Finally, he looked up again, but he didn't look at her as he said, "Your dad was driving. He was backing up the car after church, and he didn't see. Jeffrey — your father — he was just a kid. He was a kid. You understand that? He didn't want to stay for the pot-luck, so he took the keys and . . ."

So now she knew. "That's how Daniel died?"

"He was six years old."

Anna June looked into the water. She thought she saw something yellow. "How come nobody told me before now?"

"Because your grandma decided we would never talk about it. Ever. We weren't allowed to even say his name. She got rid of all the pictures of him. I told Tim when he was about your age. I thought he'd have told you by now."

"He didn't."

"First time he's kept a secret in his life."

Anna June was quiet for a few seconds. "Is that why my dad's the way he is?"

"It's hard to say about a thing like that. I don't suppose it helped matters."

Anna June watched the path the moon made across the water. She thought about walking on that path as she asked Uncle Jonathan why Grandpa hadn't ever told her.

"He was honoring your grandma's wishes. He always honored her wishes, even if it wasn't always the best thing."

Anna June looked as far down as she could into the water, which wasn't far, since it was dark and the water was muddy. She wanted to see the yellow car. And then she did see it. It was like new. She saw Daniel sitting in the backseat. The windows were all rolled down, and he was asleep. He didn't know what had happened to him.

She knew tomorrow she would go home and make a permanent card. It would be a card for her family. She would write at the top. "The True Secret History of the Haven Grebel Family." She would use her best handwriting to make the card. Later she would go to the newspaper office and do her research, and she would know how to write their story.

"Anna June," Uncle Jonathan said. His voice was serious. "I don't want to tell you what to do. I know those cards mean a lot to you." She felt embarrassed when he said that because it seemed like he knew what she'd been thinking. "But," he went on, "like you said earlier, the stories are all in your head. You won't forget them. It might not be worth fighting with your grandma over those cards." He was quiet for a few seconds before he said, "Would you maybe give it some thought?" He didn't wait for her to answer. He said, "I know you will. I know you love your grandma. And she isn't going to change her mind. She'll never change her mind once it's made up."

Anna June knew it was true what Uncle Jonathan said about Grandma. She looked across the pond at the hedge of angels. She understood why Grandpa had worked so hard with her to make it. It had been for Daniel. Grandpa had loved Daniel. He'd loved her. He'd loved Grandma. He'd loved Uncle Jonathan and Daddy. He'd loved everyone, and he would never, ever, have hurt any of them. It made tears come to her eyes to think about how sad he would be about Grandma being upset.

Uncle Jonathan saw her looking at the hedge of angels. "How many more do you need?"

"Three. I need twenty-two for Ezekiel 22."

Jonathan nodded. "I see where Dad's been firing the clay. Before I leave, I'll ask Eddie to help you."

"Grandpa helped me make them strong," she said, but she didn't tell Uncle Jonathan that she wasn't comfortable with Eddie helping. The angels were Grandpa's and her secret.

They sat together on the bank of the pond, watching the water lapping at the shore. Anna June thought about the yellow Pontiac. Poor Daddy, she thought. Poor Grandma. Poor Grandpa. Poor Uncle Jonathan. Poor, poor Daniel. The memories caught in the grass of the pasture thrummed around her. She could hear them telling her the stories of this place, the secrets no one would ever tell. Uncle Jonathan was right. She didn't need the cards. She'd give them to Grandma first thing in the morning. She wouldn't make a card for the secret history of their family after all. She didn't need to.

When she looked back into the pond, she couldn't see the yellow Pontiac anymore, but she imagined Daniel was still there asleep in the backseat, only now he was smiling. He was smiling at her.

JULY 9, 2009

She and Haven were in the habit of waking each morning at four thirty and talking together in bed for an hour before they rose for the day. For a blissful second this morning — despite the terrible dream she'd had of being in a capsized boat — Elsa woke at four thirty expecting to hear Haven wish her a good morning. Instead, she turned to see Anna June sleeping beside her, arms and legs akimbo, and, because of his soft snoring, she remembered Timothy on the floor in his sleeping bag.

Elsa dressed quietly, standing in front of the mirror only long enough to put her hair into a bun and to pin in place her prayer veil. In the kitchen, blessed quiet for a few minutes as she started a pot of coffee. She cherished this time alone while she watched for the first hint of morning light in the east. A ghostly moon hovered on the western horizon, and the constellations were still legible in that part of the sky.

As she did each morning, Elsa read her devotional from the *Martyr's Mirror*. Her copy had belonged to her mother, and she was especially soothed this morning by the notes Mama had made in the margins. All these years later it felt like a conversation with her mother. None of her sisters knew she had Mama's

Martyr's Mirror. At first Elsa had felt deceitful keeping it from them; they'd all been so troubled by its disappearance after Mama had died. When Elsa had eventually found it under Marian's bed during Marian's final illness, she'd thought it was peculiar, but she'd decided it was hers to keep. After all, she'd taken care of Marian in the end when none of the others would. She supposed by not telling her sisters, she'd also been protecting Marian's memory, knowing full well what they would have made of her hiding it that way when she'd known they'd wanted it so.

She knew the stories of the martyrs like she knew the stories of her own family. As a child, it had seemed to Elsa, when she'd first heard the stories of the martyrs, that everyone she knew and loved would die a terrible death, including her. Such suffering was the outcome of living the faith. She had expected to be tormented. Horribly. When that never happened, she'd sometimes wondered if she was really worthy of being called a Mennonite. She had carried that concern well into adulthood, wondering often if she would have the strength to suffer and still remain true to the Lord.

Haven had suffered for his faith. He'd written in his letters home about how he and the others who were doing their voluntary war service were mocked and jeered on their long journey across the country. They were called cowards and worse, and on a few occasions they were threatened with violence. Haven had said at the time there was a mob mentality afoot, that the whole country felt like a tinderbox ready to explode without much provocation. He'd been most surprised, he confessed to Elsa after he came home, by the behavior of even well-dressed ladies who had called them vile names and sometimes even spit on him and the other Mennonite brothers as they stopped along the way to Virginia.

Elsa never tired of the martyrs' stories, all the ways the saints were tested and remained faithful to their practice of adult baptism and the habit of nonviolence even in the face of terrible persecution. The martyrs had shocked and humbled their persecutors all those centuries ago by witnessing to the Lord's revelation even as they were being slain for their faith. Those who witnessed their deaths recounted how the faces of the saints were made beatific in their suffering, and many came to the Lord because of their testimony. The saints reached so many converts at their deaths that the prosecuting officials began to gag them before putting them to the stake, and when that failed, they clamped their tongues or cut them clean off. They could stop their tongues, but they couldn't snuff out the light of love and forgiveness in their eyes.

Elsa turned this morning to the story of Dirk Willems, her favorite of the martyr's testaments. It was the story she went to for courage when she felt especially tried by disappointment, as she did this morning. Willems had enacted most nobly the Mennonite doctrine of nonresistance by saving from drowning the very man who was pursuing him for the crime of adult baptism. Willems knew full well, despite his generosity in saving that man, he himself would be taken into custody and put to death, which was what came to pass. As Elsa read the story again this morning, she prayed for purity of heart in dealing with her own enemies. "Love thy enemies," Christ had commanded. "Do good unto those who wish you harm."

She and Haven had often talked about a church purified. They'd never stopped hoping for the day when all differences among their Mennonite sisters and brothers would be resolved. They longed for the day when the Lord would return to find his church prepared to meet Him as a bride is prepared to meet her groom. Over the years their little congregation had experienced its share of factions, some of them resulting in splits.

How those splits had hurt Haven. It had troubled him so, that believers could allow small differences to divide them, that the brethren would sever their relationships with one another over pride. He'd been brought low sometimes when his mediations too often failed.

Still, it was the responsibility of the faithful to preserve their precious doctrine, handed down to them for over five hundred years, from watered-down interpretations. It was their duty to be vigilant against false prophecy and the spirit of negativity. The Lord wasn't only betrayed once by His disciples. Christ was crucified again each time a believer failed Him. Elsa wanted nothing in her walk with the Lord to cause Him more suffering.

She continued to meditate on these things as she went out to feed the chickens. Red was already awake. When he saw her, he shook himself and began to strut. He threw back his head to crow. The day had officially begun.

Grandma was already gone when Anna June woke up. Timothy was still asleep on the floor, his hair all over the place, looking stupid with his mouth hanging open. Anna June dressed fast and walked home. She'd hidden her cards in the trunk of Daddy's old car, and when she came into the house for the keys, Daddy was still sleeping in the chair in front of the TV, where he slept every night. Her mom was gone somewhere, so Anna June cut a piece of banana bread from a loaf on the kitchen counter for breakfast. The house was a mess because Mom had been gone nonstop.

Anna June had been thinking about how it would be once everybody left after the funeral. She still wanted to be a farmer when she grew up, and she was worried about how she'd learn the things she needed to without Grandpa. Grandma said she would keep the farm going, but when Anna June thought about it, she knew it wasn't true. Grandma would put everything in boxes. She would get a house in town. Anna June could see it all, how Grandma would leave the house one day, and when she turned the key in the lock, it would be like a catch in her heart, and she would die too. The farm would go away because nobody could keep it. They wouldn't understand about Anna June. "You're just a kid," they'd say. "Too bad you're not older; too bad you're not a boy, so you could take over for your grandma."

"Do I have to go to school?" she'd asked Daddy one time. "Can't I stay home and work on the farm with Grandpa?"

Daddy had laughed at her. "You silly kid. You really like the farm, don't you?" He shook his head. "I hope you'll get as far away from here as you can. And, no, you can't not go to school. Why do you ask such silly questions?" She wished she could have been homeschooled by Grandpa. School was boring. Church was boring. Her family, except Grandpa, and sometimes Timothy and Daddy, was boring.

This morning as she took the box of cards out of the trunk, she felt sad thinking about the secret history. She'd worked hard on the cards. She sat down right there on the floor of the garage, not even caring about the dirt, and read through the cards. Some of the old ones looked funny to her now. She hadn't realized that a person could be embarrassed by herself until she saw her bad handwriting from when she was little. She read the story of how the Schweitzer's daughter had disappeared when she was fifteen and they didn't know if she was alive or dead. "Her name was Rosemary," she'd written, and had gone on to write, "No one ever says her name. They have seven kids, counting Rosemary, but when they talk about their kids, they never mention her. They say they have six kids."

There was the card about how the old minister's wife left him and their kids and married a man who worked at the post office in Seward. "She ran away with him to Iowa."

A card about how when the three Eggleston boys were teenagers, they shot a bunch of farmers' cows just for fun and how "for a long time everyone thought it was English boys who were doing it. When they found out who it really was, the church brethren were all sad. Those boys had to work a long time to pay back the farmers."

A card with the story of how Jacob Miller was sent to jail "for stealing things from a neighbor's house when he was young." Now Jacob Miller was an old man. He was an elder in the church and the strictest of them all. He acted like he'd never done anything wrong when he was young. Anna June had told Daddy, "The elders should say they were bad. That would be better. Now they act like they're so good, like they were never bad. No one listens to them."

The cards had helped Anna June know things, like how she shouldn't run away from home the way Fred Stutzman did when he was a kid because your parents look and look for you, and they imagine you got killed or maybe you killed someone, and then they make up their own story about what happened, and when you do come home they still believe a little what they made up about you, and you're an outcast.

Or you shouldn't go around with English boys like Margaret Yoder, who got pregnant before she was married and the boy didn't marry her. And then she had to drop out of school and take care of her daughter, who's older than Anna June's dad now but when she was young got teased a lot because of her mom.

You shouldn't talk too much because that's how the minister, Mr. Denckelman, and his family got run off from another church. Grandma said, "That man would try the patience of Job."

So, Anna June knew some things because of that. Sometimes in church Anna June whispered, "Rosemary," just so no one forgot her name.

She remembered this morning how when she was little she had wanted to fly. She had thought God would give her whatever she wanted if she prayed for it. She prayed behind Grandpa and Grandma's barn, and that's when she started preaching.

163

She preached like the preacher she'd seen on TV. He walked back and forth and asked lots of questions, and he got louder and louder. After she prayed to fly, she started walking back and forth like that.

She had wanted to be a preacher for a while, but Grandma had looked at her with a frown on her face when she found her behind the barn. "I don't know where you get these notions of yours," Grandma had said. Anna June didn't tell her about the TV or wanting to fly. Grandma wouldn't have liked that. She didn't approve of watching TV. She scolded Anna June, but she never scolded Daddy, and he was the one who watched TV 24-7. When Anna June told her mom it wasn't fair, her mom shushed her and said, "Nothing's fair. Nothing in this life is fair," and that was when Anna June knew God was never going to let her fly, and she started helping Grandpa in her spare time because he needed her. And she started helping Grandma with the history.

"Morning, Mrs. Grebel." Eddie took off his cap as he approached the chicken yard.

"You're up early this morning, Eddie," she said.

"I wanted to get a look at things after the storm."

"Well?"

"Everything's fine."

"That's a relief. Thank you for checking on that for me, Eddie." She paused a moment. "And thank you for having them put the tractor back over behind the corncrib like you did yesterday. That was thoughtful of you."

Eddie's brows drew down. "I'm afraid I didn't have anything to do with that, ma'am."

Elsa covered her surprise at hearing this by going on to ask about how the rest of the county had fared in the storm.

"Not so good," Eddie said. "I took the long way around on my way over here, and there's serious damage. Everything along the Blue is flooded, and not all that far west of us, as close as the Jantzens, all the corn is down, and the beans are flattened."

"Oh dear."

Eddie shifted from foot to foot. He seemed shy about talking to her, but he went on anyway. "It's a sad sight," he said. "I heard last night the governor announced a state of emergency in parts of Seward and York counties."

Elsa shook her head. It was hard to believe this morning, with the birds singing and the wind so still, that there could be such trouble nearby.

"I'll get to work now, unless you have something else you need, Mrs. Grebel."

"No, you go on ahead. You'll be at the viewing tonight, won't you?"

Eddie nodded and replaced his cap. He looked down a moment. He was a young man, and she noticed now how handsome he was. You got so used to a person, you didn't even look at them anymore. She figured he probably had a girlfriend, though Elsa had never seen him with a girl in church. He was a quiet boy, the youngest of the Hoffman kids. He'd worked for Haven for two years, eaten at her table most days for lunch, and she didn't know a thing about him, except that he was a good kid and that he always ate what was put in front of him and thanked her afterward and offered to clear his own plate.

Something in his face told her he'd never been this close to death before. She could see it frightened him, but she didn't know what she could say to help him. As the sun came over the horizon, the sky was suddenly a brilliant blue. Dark-blue clouds freckled the sky toward the west, and along the horizon they formed small peaks so that they looked like a mountain range in the distance.

"What should I wear for the viewing tonight?" Nina said when she woke up that morning.

"I'm wearing a jacket and tie." Jonathan, who had been awake for a while, was reading in a chair beside the window.

Nina sat up. She pulled her heavy hair off her neck. "Okay. Anything else I need to know about this thing?"

"No," Jonathan said putting his book away. "There won't be a service tonight. It's just a chance for people to gather before the funeral tomorrow." Nina's Unitarian family eschewed almost all ritual. Jonathan had once heard her mother complain that the Unitarian Church services were too churchy for her. Nina had never been to a Mennonite church service with him, but he knew how she'd behave. She'd be like an ethnographer, watching the strange death rituals of a foreign culture. She'd appreciate the simplicity of the service. No pomp. Nothing decorative or stylized. No liturgical language. No priestly garb. No incense. Nothing to stand between the worshipper and God. Church services were as much an opportunity for fellowship as for instruction, and each service allowed for the congregation to question and speak back to the sermon. She'd like that too. Afterward she'd be full of questions for him.

"I'm glad you're here," Jonathan said as he stood and leaned to kiss her on the forehead. In her place he knew he wouldn't be as generous. He was glad her family had low expectations of him. Her mother and her two sisters stayed in constant contact with one another by phone and saw one another at least once a week. There were always little feuds and squabbles among the sisters, constant reassessments and realignments. It wore him out sometimes just hearing about it. Of the sisters Nina was the least high maintenance. They gathered only rarely as a family, for one holiday or another. After dinner the husbands offered to clean up the dishes and then did their best to stay out of the way of the women until it was time to leave.

Tim was on the front porch when later Jonathan took his coffee outside. They sat for a few minutes in silence, enjoying the morning. The crickets were out, as were the birds: meadowlarks and cardinals, blackbirds and jays, sparrows and robins, and red-headed woodpeckers. Now and then a mourning dove cooed. This morning Jonathan studied his mother's flower garden. She spent hours each summer day tending it and the vegetable garden, and it showed. It was a true prairie garden, containing both native grasses and flowers: little and big bluestem, side oats, prairie coneflowers, Husker penstemon, speedwell and yellow yarrow, old-fashioned tiger lilies, iris, rudbeckia, sedum, black-eyed Susans, sunflowers, and hollyhocks. In the shade were hosta and bishop's goutweed, astilbe, and lily of the valley. She had flowering crabapple trees and redbuds and whitebuds, serviceberry and chokecherry. There was something always in bloom.

The sky was blandly blue this morning, looking innocent after the storm the day before. The local newspaper was full of accounts of the devastation across the county: entire fields wiped out by straight winds, trees uprooted, and rooftops ripped away from houses.

168

His father's fields had been untouched. Jonathan had taken the truck out that morning to see for himself, not entirely trusting Eddie's report, though he couldn't say why. Eddie was as dependable a hand as you could want.

Tim interrupted his thoughts as he slapped at a mosquito. "Don't blame me, Pop," he said as he stretched his long legs out in front of him. For a second Jonathan thought Tim was taking responsibility for the wreckage of the storm, until he realized he was referring to the situation between his mother and Anna June. Jonathan still wasn't sure what role Tim had played in his mother's shunning of Anna June, but he guessed he'd done his share.

Jonathan's preferred way of dealing with Tim was to keep a wary distance. He was the one stray Nina had tried to love and finally declared a "hard case." Her word, not Jonathan's.

Seeing the limitations of his own provincial life, Jonathan had tried to give Tim every opportunity he hadn't had. Once he had met Karalee, Jonathan transferred all the passionate faith fever of his youth, all his former desire to be a martyr for the faith, into living life as fully as he could. He didn't regret any of those years, even if some of it — especially after the split with Karalee — had gone toward excess. One of his girlfriends had once told him he "had a powerful death wish," but the truth was before that, in his earlier life, Jonathan's faith had been a death wish. The church valorized the martyrs and instructed believers to curb every natural impulse. Raised to be fearful of sin, as an adolescent he'd seen experience as something dangerous, something to be avoided.

No, by the time Jonathan left the church, he'd decided to live his life as deeply as he could, and as Tim got older, he'd wanted him to be exposed to all the experiences he'd been kept from in his own confined childhood; he'd wanted Tim to have every option possible for his life. Jonathan still believed the more you knew, the better you could make the right decision about how to live your own life.

"What's the story then, Tim?" he said now.

"That's complicated."

"So boil it down for me."

"You know Elsa," Tim said, using her first name, as he always did when talking to him, which for some reason irked Jonathan. Tim went on, "She hears something, and she runs with it. You know how she is."

Yes, he did know how she was. For once, Jonathan realized, Tim probably hadn't been trying to be a shit disturber; it was just his default mode. Without even trying, he'd created a crisis.

"Pop, I know you won't believe me," Tim went on, "but Elsa's the one person in the world I really wouldn't want to hurt."

Jonathan felt a sting that he'd been excluded from Tim's concern. And Tim, who'd always had an uncanny way of knowing what Jonathan was thinking, went for the tender spot now. "Don't take it like that, Pop. It's not like we were ever that close when I was growing up. I mean, I'm past all that now, but still."

Jonathan was silent.

"Come on, Pop. I didn't mean anything by it. It's just the past. It's how things were."

He had to marvel at Tim's dexterity in bringing a conversation that had begun with a question of his possible wrongdoing to focus instead on Jonathan's past mistakes. He chose to ignore it and said, "Tim, if you're in any way fanning the flame here—"

"Jesus, Pop. What are you trying to say?"

"If you're exacerbating the probl——"

"I can't believe you. You know that. You're so quick to believe the worst about me. What's with that?"

"Settle down, son," Jonathan said, hearing as he said it his father's voice.

170

Tim heard it too. "Don't ever go there," he said, his voice flat and cold. "You don't have the right to go there. Gramps was —" Tim stood up without finishing and went inside. Jonathan sipped his coffee. He thought about going after him but decided it would probably only make things worse.

From inside the house he heard a sudden burst of laughter and the murmuring of voices as people gathered for the day. His parents had many friends, and Jonathan couldn't help wondering this morning who would come to his own funeral. Monty. Their neighbors Joel and Karen, Nina's family. That would be it. Maybe a few of his former clients, a few colleagues in the industry. Some of Nina's friends from work and former students would come to support her. People she'd served with on boards and committees. Truth was, Nina had many connections in the city that didn't interest him. He couldn't help but note the omission of his own family at that gathering. Oh, sure. Tim would be there, but Jeffrey? The aunts? Jonathan wasn't feeling sorry for himself. Quite the contrary — he was relieved there wouldn't be such a spectacle at his own death.

He decided to pick a few tiger lilies growing along the fence to take in to Nina.

"Oh good," she said as he came into their room. "What do you think about this dress for tonight?" She held up a black dress still on its hanger.

"That'll be perfect," Jonathan said and handed her the flowers.

"How nice. Where did you get these?" He gestured with his head toward the yard. "Oh no," Nina said, looking at the flowers like they'd suddenly become a problem.

"Don't worry. She won't even notice they're gone."

"Are you kidding?" Nina set the flowers aside before slipping on the dress and looking at herself in the mirror. "You're sure this will be all right?" She turned toward him. Nina rarely dressed up, and when she did, she looked elegant in a way that always surprised him. She swept her hair up now into a loose bun and pinned it. "I don't want to be inappropriate," she said. "Will this bother anyone?"

"You're going to bother someone plenty," he said with a smile. She laughed and pushed him away. "Don't worry, Nina," Jonathan said. "I meant it when I said they have low expectations for outsiders. Just be yourself."

Nina took off the dress and hung it up again before pulling on her customary summer outfit: loose linen pants and a linen shirt. She looked at herself soberly in the mirror again as she put on her silver hoop earrings.

"Sweetie," Jonathan said, "we should talk."

She looked at him through the vanity mirror and, sensing his seriousness, turned around to look at him, her hand still raised to her ear. "What's the matter?"

"Nothing's the matter," Jonathan said. "We just need to talk, and I don't want you to take it the wrong way." Nina raised her eyebrows, her signal that he should go on as she finished putting on the earring back. He motioned for her to come sit beside him on the bed.

When she did, he put his arm around her. "Nina, I know you have only the best intentions toward Anna June, but, babe, Jeffrey and Kathy, they aren't going to understand this scheme of yours and Mother's about Anna June going to school in Boston."

"Why wouldn't they want what's best for her?"

"Nina. Who's to say what's best? I don't think they'd agree that Anna June is deprived—"

"But—"

"No buts. They don't see the world the way we do. You know that."

"I do know that, but once we lay out what we can offer her

in Boston, once Anna June comes around, and she's starting to, Jonathan. She's starting to talk to me."

"Nina. Don't get ahead of yourself."

"But your mother — "

"My mother has ulterior motives, and we don't need to get caught in the middle." At this Nina sighed. "I'm not trying to be a naysayer," Jonathan hurried to say, knowing how much she loathed naysayers. "But if we want to help Anna June, we'll have to find another way. She's just a kid, Nina, and Jeffrey and Kathy aren't going to give her up any more than we would have given up a child of ours."

Jonathan could see by the change in Nina's expression, this last point made sense to her. He could tell she was disappointed, though. Without her saying it, he knew she'd been setting up a room for Anna June in the house. He thought he knew which room it was, the one on the third floor Nina always said would have been her bedroom if she'd lived there when she was a girl.

"Okay," she said and stood up from the bed. "Okay."

Anna June was careful not to let Timothy, the sneak, know she was in the attic. She opened the old trunk in the corner. There were letters on the bottom, and she could see they were old. Some were addressed to Grandpa and some to Grandma. She was curious about the letters, but that wasn't what she was looking for. She dug deeper and found papers: a marriage certificate, things about the farm, and finally she found three birth certificates. She opened Daniel's. Daniel Jacob Grebel. Born December 10, 1953. Anna June looked at the birth certificate for a long time. After that she looked through the albums Timothy had shown her the day before. She looked and looked, but there wasn't a single picture of Daniel. She finally found one old picture of the whole family. Daniel was only a baby.

She looked closely at the picture. Grandma looked so happy and so pretty. They all looked happy, even her dad, who was tall and thin and looked totally different than he did now. Jonathan looked a lot the same, except his hair was black then, and now it was almost gray.

Anna June couldn't find any more pictures of Daniel. She wanted to see how he'd looked when he was a little boy. She'd been kneeling on the floor while she looked through the photo albums, but now she sat down on the cot and glanced around the room. Besides the trunk, the shelves with storage boxes, the old rocking chair, and the cot where she was sitting, there was an old mirror, taller than she was. The painted floor in the attic was dry and peeling. The air felt hot and stuffy, and she noticed the windows had been closed. Someone had thought about the rain yesterday. She figured it was probably Grandma. Grandma thought about everything. Daddy always said, "She doesn't miss much except what's right in front of her nose."

Elsa could see immediately someone had been in the attic again. Things were even more disarranged than they'd been the day before. Doggone it if it wasn't those kids. She saw where they'd been rummaging through Haven's old steamer trunk. Things had been taken out and left all over the place. She could only guess what they'd been up to. Strange how her children and grandchildren had no respect for her privacy or her property. There was a sort of marauding spirit in all of them, as though whatever was hers was theirs too. There were things in that trunk that were fragile and shouldn't be handled carelessly.

How the past came back to her in the attic, though. She felt it like a spirit in the room today, memories so palpable she could almost forget the present. She saw herself as a young woman again standing in front of the mirror across the room that had once stood in their bedroom. She remembered herself as a new bride at fifteen, crying because she was afraid of disappointing Haven at the first supper she was preparing for guests. Haven had come to stand behind her that day so they'd been framed together in the mirror. They'd made a handsome couple. He had towered above her as he laid his hands on her shoulders. "Look at yourself, Elsa."

She had looked at him in the mirror. "Not me, Elsa. Yourself. Look at yourself," Haven had said. And she had, feeling how her eyes wanted to skitter away from the image. Marian had warned her against vanity and had been critical about girls who spent too many hours in front of the mirror, but Elsa had made herself look that day, and when she had, Haven said, "I've just married the most beautiful, the sweetest, girl in five states. There is nothing, nothing you could do, Elsa, to embarrass me except not respect yourself and fail in your faith." She had cried again when he said that, but from that day forward she'd always felt Haven's warm hands on her shoulders, giving her confidence.

All of his letters from his two years in Virginia were in that trunk too. She hoped the kids hadn't disturbed them. He'd served along with the young men from her home church in Kansas, and what they saw in that hospital for the mentally ill shocked them. People treated far worse than animals. A hell on earth, they'd said. The boys she knew from home had gone back to Kansas committed to making a change, and together they'd started, those boys, the Menninger Clinic. She'd been proud of them for their work.

She remembered, though, how Haven had raised all sorts of troubling questions in his letters to her about the doctrine of peace and what it meant to let other men fight and die so they could live their faith.

"In the years of the young church," she remembered him writing once, "resisting conscription meant certain imprisonment, even death. Refusing to bear arms came with a high price. But now? Can those same doctrines apply when the stakes have changed so? Is it right to let other men fight and risk death so we are free to object without paying that high price?"

Elsa remembered feeling at the time he was paying a high price being so far away from her for so long, and so soon after they'd married. And she remembered feeling queasy as she'd read his letters. Had she married an infidel? Would he turn out to be like her beloved, rebellious brother, Zeke, someone who would disgrace the family and the faith by putting on the uniform of a soldier, taking up arms in defense of a worldly government, to resist an enemy with force rather than love them as Christ had commanded?

Elsa had written back to Haven that the Lord had spoken through the blood of their martyred ancestors. How could they question such a hard-won doctrine? She'd scolded him. Poor boy. He and the others had only been boys when they'd had to make those terrible choices. She could see that now. And she, who was spared the consequences of such a decision, had yet been so confident of the answers. It pained her now to think of it. What had she known?

And Zeke, dying there in battle the way he had, her last words to him that she loved him but she feared for his eternal soul, his last letter in response to hers, a short "Don't fear for me, Sister. Fear for yourself." What a rebuke she'd felt in that letter from a brother who had moved so far beyond her and the family that had disowned him. Only Haven, among all of them, had tried to understand Zeke's decision.

Haven had finally made peace with himself, deciding the Lord had called him and the other Mennonite brothers who did not fight to a hard faith. But still, Haven had told her, he respected Zeke's decision all the same.

When years later Elsa was tested, there would be no consoling letters from Haven. There'd be no word spoken. He'd tried, she supposed, to reach her, but she hadn't wanted his help. She had felt herself far out on an unknown sea—she, who had only seen the ocean a few times in her life—yet she'd felt it vividly how far she'd moved away from the familiar shore, moved beyond her family, beyond humanity itself and into a strange nether sea. Only with God's grace had she returned.

For the second time in her life now, she felt desperate for the comfort of Scripture, for the inspiration she usually took from the *Martyr's Mirror*, but she couldn't seem to hold for long a coherent thought. She started now with the beatitudes, "Blessed are the meek," and before she could finish that Scripture she'd moved on to 1 Corinthians, "When I was a child, I thought as a child" and ended with "In a twinkling, we shall be changed." For two days now she'd been shuffling from scripture to scripture like this, unable to see anything through. She'd listened to what wisdom others had to share, tried to grasp what they were saying, but her mind remained slippery and blank. She felt almost desperate for the Lord's word, needed it like she needed air to breath, needed it to help her stitch her life back together, but there was some barrier to understanding, some resistance to what she had always known and trusted in her faith.

Words didn't quite make sense as they once had. Among the fragments that had been repeating all day were those familiar verses from Ecclesiastes: "For everything there is a purpose under heaven. A time to be born, a time to die." This was how she had lived her life, understanding not by the date on the calendar but by the direction of the sun, the feel of the wind, the texture of the soil and the air, the changes in birdsong and the habits of God's other creatures when to start the garden and when to harvest, when to order chicks and when to slaughter the fryers.

Even Haven's death, as terrible as it was, did not feel unnatural to her. He had lived his full measure and more. They had talked about it, as all older couples surely do. While he hadn't agreed with her about being prepared financially, just as he hadn't agreed with her about many things over the years, she had known this day would come.

What she needed most now was to return to the quiet simplicity of her life. Only then would she be able to assess her own mind. She couldn't tolerate the constant human traffic, the insistence on small talk, the forever sitting around.

She had hard work ahead of her. Grieving was as exhausting physically as it was mentally. She knew she couldn't put off forever the great heaving sadness ahead of her as she realized fully in the days to come what it would mean to never see Haven again in this life. She would feel it most when she boxed up his things, and yet she looked forward to that work. She welcomed the orderliness of such tasks, the necessity of facing her changed reality. What she couldn't stand now was the waiting.

Downstairs there was such a din in the house she could hear it all the way up here. Emily's loud laugh, the hum of many conversations, the kitchen door opening and slamming shut, pots and pans and silverware clanking and crashing as someone washed dishes yet again, the sound of the water in the pipes as the toilet flushed, footsteps inside and car tires on the gravel outside as cars came and went. The meaning of all this activity completely eluded Elsa for a few seconds, and she thought of humans with the same detachment she usually reserved for insects, whose busyness seemed random and slightly foolish to the human eye.

It was so unexpected, this thought, that Elsa didn't see the blasphemy of it right away, but now she did. Here they were, creatures made in God's own image, creatures for whom the Creation had been made and for whom Christ's sacrifice had been poured out, and she'd had the nerve to compare them to insects? She couldn't imagine where such a thought had come from. Of course there was meaning in their actions. Of course God accepted their praise and their worship as something vital. They'd been created to praise and worship Him. He cared for both the sinner and the saint. He loved them all. He offered

His salvation to everyone. There wasn't a human on this earth who wasn't precious in His sight. Elsa said a quick prayer for forgiveness.

She smiled, though, as she recalled what Haven had always called the summer evening nature clock band. "At seven," he said, "the mourning doves begin to blow their oboes. By eight the cicada join in with their rusty saws, and by nine the crickets come out with their castanets." Ever since he'd told her this, Elsa could tell the time on summer nights. She had the idea then for a new quilt pattern, one featuring insects. She could see how she might capture the muscularity of the grasshopper, the elegance of the praying mantis, the rotundity of the bumblebee and the sleekness of the wasp and the hornet, the compactness of the fly. She decided she wouldn't try to include the mosquito, the only one of god's creatures she couldn't see any point to at all.

She'd look through her fabric room once things settled down, think some more about a pattern. She fantasized for a few seconds about the luxury of going to a quilting store and buying the colors and fabrics she wanted. She'd only been in a quilting store one time in her life, having always used leftover fabric for her quilts. The experience of seeing shelf upon shelf filled with beautiful fabrics, all lying together, had left her flushed and overcome with a kind of desire she'd never felt before, the wish to possess all those colors and textures and designs. It had been such an overpowering experience of greed she'd avoided such stores ever since.

Without fail, every time Jonathan walked into the kitchen, the aunts pressed more food upon him, and he couldn't seem to get enough. Here were all the things he and Nina wouldn't have in their house, the comfort food he'd grown up with and craved, sometimes even dreaming about meals like this, eating ravenously in his dreams: sliced ham, scalloped potato casserole, bologna, summer sausage, and fried chicken. Cheese. White bread and mayo. Butter. Cream. Bacon. Whipped cream. Brownies. Coconut cream pie. Carrot cake with cream cheese frosting. Deviled eggs. He couldn't even pretend to resist. With every invitation to eat, he accepted.

This morning, as he sat at the kitchen table eating a second breakfast, he heard a tattletaling story from the aunts about how his mother still refused to eat a thing. He reminded them, "She's never been a big eater," to which the aunts all shook their heads. "That Marian," they said. "She learned that from Marian." His mother had apparently learned a lot of things from Marian, and for the first time this morning Jonathan became aware of the rift his grandfather's second marriage had caused in the family. "Only two months after Mama died," they told him, "us older girls were managing just fine, and he had to go and do that." They skirted around it, but he heard between the lines Marian's harsh ways, her bitterness toward their mother, and her cruelty, especially to the two youngest children, Elsa and Zeke. They were all convinced the reason Zeke had joined the army was to get away from home.

"He wanted to get as far away from Marian as he could," Emily said, and the others nodded.

"Father stayed away plenty himself," Eleanor said, at which the other two giggled.

"Isn't that the truth," Emily said.

"We'd warned him," Evelyn told Jonathan.

As they talked, Jonathan looked around for his mother. He didn't see her anywhere, and Aunt Emily gestured up with her head to indicate she was in the attic again. Like an injured animal going away to clean its wounds, she kept running off. Jonathan could barely stand that whiny thing she'd been doing the last two days — telling everyone how his father had given away everything they'd ever earned, leaving her now with nothing — before adding the ubiquitous "God will provide" routine. It was getting tiresome, all made-to-order, though, the way she went on and on about it. The whole deal. Made-to-order. The truth was, his father had left her with a small fortune, but she couldn't seem to hear it. She'd always been irrational to the core, never letting her beliefs in any way be compromised by reality.

He was ready to go home. All morning he'd been thinking about the comforts of their house in Boston. He wanted his fresh ground Peets coffee. He wanted to sit in the quiet of the sunroom and read his *New York Times* and his *Globe*. He wanted to check his e-mails and take a shower in his own bathroom, instead of having to share one bathroom with a houseful of people.

He suddenly wished they'd brought Lolita with them. He was

worried about her so far away. She was old and diabetic, and he was the one who administered her insulin shots every day. She was fine with the house sitter, he knew, but he'd have felt better having her here with them. The cats would be picking on her. If something happened to that little dog while they were gone, he didn't think he'd ever forgive himself.

The older he got, the less he liked to be away from home, the irony of which didn't escape him, since when he'd been younger, he got antsy if he stayed in one place too long. By the time he and Nina had bought the house in JP, though, he'd been ready to settle down. They'd bought at the right time, and their house was worth a fortune now, even with the recent drop in real estate values. Jonathan had tried telling this to his father one time, but his father had only looked at Jonathan with those fish eyes of his. None of that mattered to him, and he hadn't understood why it mattered to Jonathan. To Haven Grebel a man was only worth as much as he could give to others.

His parents had never been interested in Jonathan's work, his graduate degrees, the two design books he'd published, the work he'd done in some of the finest houses and institutions in Boston. They'd come to visit him there only once, while he'd been living in an artist's co-op in the South End. His dad had insisted on renting a car then spent the entire week bewildered by Boston's streets and nervous about its drivers. His parents had been uncomfortable and out of place the entire time. Jonathan couldn't help but take it personally the way they couldn't seem to adapt to Boston or his life there. They'd never come back, and he'd been glad for it. Not only had they been unimpressed with his apartment, but they'd seemed offended by his things, studiously avoiding the paintings and other pieces of art in the studio spaces of the collective.

Jonathan wished he could blame it on their ignorance, but he knew it wasn't that simple. They'd both traveled, especially his father. No, their implied criticism was much bigger than that; it was about scarce resources, rich Westerners in a world of need. It was what they perceived as self-indulgence, both in the arts and in his choice of work, lighting options for expensive restaurants, hotels, and wealthy homes. If he stripped away the religious doctrine, their austere beliefs and practice of sustainability weren't all that different from the most eco-conscious of his friends, and some of that same judgmental sanctimoniousness made both arguments equally tiresome.

"Why don't you go up and talk to your mother, " Evelyn said now as she took his empty plate away. Her suggestion startled him. No way would he interrupt his mother's privacy. He felt certain she thought no one had noticed her going up to the attic. How well could her sisters know his mother to even suggest he do such a thing?

Grandma was vacuuming the living room rug when Anna June got back to her house. Aunt Evelyn was telling her to stop and let someone else do it, but Grandma kept waving Aunt Evelyn away. Anna June waited until Grandma was finished. As Grandma shut off the vacuum, she saw Anna June and frowned, but when Anna June held up the purple shoebox of her cards, she couldn't believe the difference in Grandma's face. Grandma smiled at her, and at the same time she looked like she might cry. She hugged Anna June and took the cards away from her without even putting away the vacuum cleaner first.

Grandma didn't say anything, but she pulled Anna June after her. On their way outside, she took a matchbook from one of the kitchen drawers. Anna June followed her to the burn barrel out by the workshop, where Grandma took out a folded newspaper and held the matches out to Anna June. She nodded for Anna June to light the paper on fire. Once she'd done that, Grandma threw more paper into the barrel.

They watched together as the paper burned. The fire popped as Grandma added kindling. After a while, once she had a good fire going, she motioned for Anna June to throw the box of cards onto it. Anna June couldn't do it right away. She held onto the box and thought about all the stories again.

Some of them didn't matter and she could forget them, but some did. She wanted to remember the stories about girls, especially the silly stories, like how Emma Yoder had once gotten everyone in her fourth grade class to sign their names to a piece of paper. Even the fourth grade teacher signed the paper. After everyone had signed their names, Emma wrote across the top, "We don't like you," and gave it to a girl in her class she didn't like. Daddy had slapped his leg and laughed when he'd told Anna June that story. "That landed Emma into big trouble," he'd said. Daddy had been in Emma's class. "Made me look at old Emma in a completely different way after that. She had a little something in her for sure," he said. Whatever it was Emma Yoder had, Anna June couldn't see it in her now. She just looked like the rest of the old ladies in the church.

There'd been other pranks and funny stories, but Anna June felt sad about barely remembering them. She wished she could read all the cards one more time before she turned them over to Grandma. She hugged the box to her. Grandma frowned and motioned for her to throw it in the fire. When she finally dropped it in the flames, she heard the box snap and sizzle like it was angry to be on fire. It sounded like it didn't want to burn. The cards inside didn't want to burn either. Anna June watched as her own handwriting on the cards started to disappear, the cards turning brown around the edges then black as they started to curl up on themselves. It made her feel funny watching something that was a part of her disappearing like that.

Once the cards were turned to ashes, Anna June looked up. Grandma was watching her with a serious face. She didn't seem so happy anymore. For a long time she didn't say anything, and it made Anna June start to feel uncomfortable how Grandma was looking at her.

"Young lady," Grandma finally said, "we're going to forget about all this. We're going to forget it ever happened, and you're going to forget those stories. You understand? It's evil to repeat stories about sin and human frailty without a reason for doing so. You, young lady, have no reason and no right to repeat these things."

Anna June looked once more at the ashes. Black smoke came out of the barrel. She felt so sad she wanted to cry. She didn't, though, and it was a good thing because Grandma was still watching her. Anna June finally nodded at Grandma. She wouldn't tell her she was doing this for Grandpa and for Daniel and not because Grandma had told her to.

Nina had convinced his mother to show them some of the new quilts she'd been working on for this year's quilt auction, part of the Mennonite Relief sale held nationwide. The shades were always drawn in the quilting room and the door kept closed so that, unlike the rest of the house, the room was cool and dark. As always, there were several finished quilts neatly rolled on thick dowels. On the quilting frame was a new quilt top waiting to be finished. The quilters, his mother told them, still gathered every week to work. Both Nina and Jonathan watched as she unrolled a quilt from its dowel.

Nina gasped when she saw it. "This is exquisite. What pattern is it?"

"Oh, that's just one I made up myself," his mother said.

Nina fingered the fabric. "It's lovely." They continued to watch as his mother brought out more quilts, Nina declaring all of them works of art before going on to ask about a particular stitch or admiring the choice of a color scheme. Each time, Jonathan noticed, his mother responded by pointing out her mistakes. "I made a terrible mess here with this one" or "I shouldn't have used that green. It threw the entire thing off." There wasn't a single quilt they admired that his mother simply and graciously acknowledged with thanks.

As a boy, Jonathan had played under the quilt frame while the women of the church were gathered at their work around it. He could still picture all those bodiless legs and feet under the quilt. He'd watched his mother wallpaper this room fifty years earlier. It looked like the same wallpaper, but he was sure it wasn't. She'd always hung new wallpaper over the old every few years. He noticed she still wallpapered the ceilings the old-fashioned way. As a boy, he'd stood below the ladder and watched her work as she handled those strips of wet paper and hung them by herself on the ceilings. This wasn't the vinyl wallpaper they had now but real paper, easily torn and unwieldy when wet with paste.

His mother had always done a masterful job, and he noted today the straight edges. No bubbles or tears. He wondered, though, why she had never asked anyone for help. She'd gladly gone to help other women in the church with such household tasks, but when it came to asking for help herself, she couldn't seem to do it. She'd often complained about how difficult things were for her, a complaint wrapped in an odd sort of gratitude. "At least I can still do my own wallpapering, slaughtering chickens, putting up tomatoes" — you name it. "I work my fingers to the bone," she'd say, "but I'm thankful I have the good health I do."

His most enduring memory of his mother was of her bustling about from task to task. She hated idle hands in herself and others, and contemplation was not her strong suit. Even the ten minutes she set aside each morning for her devotions had always seemed rushed and perfunctory to him.

As far as he'd seen, she wasn't good at questioning herself either. Jonathan had once witnessed an argument between his parents. His mother, he remembered, had been insisting the month for putting up hay was May, and his father had tried without success to convince her the haying month was June, a fact everyone in farm country knew to be true. It had been an absurd argument, but instead of backing down, his mother had grown more entrenched in her insistence, until finally his father gave in, saying, "I don't know, Elsa. You're probably right. My memory isn't what it used to be."

Later in the barn, Jonathan, full of adolescent outrage, had said to his father, "How do you put up with it?" to which his father, silent for a long time, had finally stopped what he was doing, the hayfork suspended for a moment, to say, "If your mother says the sky is red, the sky is red." And to this day Jonathan didn't know if his father had said this out of love or resignation, nor for sure if there was a difference between the two after all.

His mother was talking now about the next quilt auction. She'd been in charge of the regional auction for over sixty years. Shortly after he and Nina were married, Jonathan had taken Nina, knowing she'd like it. And she had. She'd bought a quilt and still told friends in Boston about the experience of standing at the auction beside men she'd taken for down-on-their-luck Mennonite farmers who were bidding ten thousand dollars and higher on individual quilts. The money the women raised each year went to support the Disaster Relief Fund.

Until going to that auction, Nina told Jonathan, she hadn't realized how committed the church was to that cause. They'd started their relief efforts after the Second World War, when they'd sent, along with other groups, relief teams into Europe and saw the extent of the need there. The Mennonite community knew firsthand the importance to someone who had just lost everything of having things as simple as a toothbrush and toothpaste, a bar of soap and a bottle of shampoo, a washcloth and a towel. Their motto: "A cup of cold water offered in the name of love."

"Elsa, your quilts are all so elegant," Nina said as they were leaving the quilt room. "You have such an eye for color and design." As his mother turned off the light and closed the door behind them, Nina added, "I still love the quilt I bought at the auction in 1992. You probably don't remember it."

Jonathan was surprised by the look of genuine pleasure that crossed his mother's face at this. "I remember that quilt very well," she said. "It's one I made."

"I never knew that, Elsa!" Nina said. "Why didn't you tell me? That makes me so happy." At this Nina grabbed his mother into one of her big hugs. After Nina released her, his mother seemed barely able to suppress her smile.

Elsa removed Haven's and her letters from the bottom of the trunk. He'd brought them back home with him, telling her he'd been so homesick while he was away he'd read them over and over again. The paper was old and brittle. As she opened a few of the letters, the edges broke off. She was embarrassed as she read the words written by her younger self. She hadn't seen these letters since she'd put them away almost sixty-five years before.

Most of what she'd written was to report on the farm: the price of eggs and cream (they were still milking cows at the time). She'd had the help of a hired man, but she'd done much of the work herself. Haven's letters were more serious, more thoughtful. He'd always given such thought to things.

She couldn't imagine what he'd have made of Anna June's behavior the last couple of days, but she was so relieved since Anna June had turned over those cards, she felt almost happy. People could say what they wanted about how the church no longer practiced shunning, but she knew in this case it had been necessary. Of course, Haven wouldn't have agreed, she knew. He'd had a bad experience as a child with it.

All Elsa knew was that as an old man, his father had disagreed with the other church elders about the treatment of the native people in Ontario and the practice of speaking only German in church services. The old man had felt strongly the church should reach out to their neighbors in Canada, adapt to their new home and its language, and make the Gospel available to those in need. The dispute had grown rancorous, and a couple other elders convinced the congregation to shun Haven's father because of it.

The worst of it, Haven had told Elsa one time, was the expectation of the church leaders that the ban continue at home. Haven, the second youngest of the children, remembered his mother crying as she moved his father's things into the barn. His father — already old by the time he'd married and had children — was an elderly man at the time, and he wasn't allowed to eat or sleep with the family. Haven remembered how his mother begged his father to repent and how the old man had refused, only moving back into the house after he and two other men finally started another congregation.

No matter. It was over now with Anna June. Elsa had seen it through. She'd worked to bring Anna June back into good standing with the brethren and back to the Lord's grace.

In the same way, she and Haven had worked hard to make a peaceful home for their boys. They'd been a happy family when the boys were little, hadn't they? Hadn't there been laughter and singing? Hadn't they had simple fun together, fun with their boys: picking berries in the summer, hayrides in the fall, sledding in winter, pulling taffy on a winter's evening while a blizzard kept them inside? On those cold nights before they had central heat, they had sometimes slept on the living room floor, close to the wood-burning stove. Those nights Haven told stories about his childhood in Canada and the characters he'd known there. As he spoke, his voice took on the northern brogue of his upbringing. He was a good mimic, and he could imitate the various types that had made up the Canadian backwoods. Elsa could still see the boys laughing, their bright little faces watching Haven's every move. How they'd adored their father, those boys.

Haven had been angry at her after what happened, angrier than he'd ever been. He hadn't understood. She'd told him so, and he'd said in response, "I understand very well, Elsa. You'll be the architect of a monument to grief. That's all there will be left of us if you keep on as you are." She didn't want to think about that now. He'd been so unfair to her. And what he'd said had been untrue. After all, she'd been the one to hold the family together, and she was glad she'd had the strength to carry on as she had. Haven had been wrong about that, but they'd gotten past it. All of them had. That was long ago in the past.

Still, she'd never told anyone how she'd plotted for a few months that winter to leave the family. She'd saved some egg money, and she'd concluded her life with Haven was over. She'd even gone so far as to pack a few things in a suitcase she kept in the back of the closet. For a while she'd wanted nothing so much as to forget everything and everyone. She had no idea where she'd planned to go, only that she longed to be somewhere far away.

Jonathan had enough e-mails that needed a longer response he decided to try to find a computer somewhere. He had low expectations as he went into the Bethel town library but was surprised to find a bank of new computers along one wall. All of them were occupied, and he signed up to wait his turn. The librarian, a younger woman he didn't recognize, told him he'd have forty-five minutes when his turn came. She looked at his name after he'd signed in. "Are you Haven's son?" When Jonathan said he was, she went on, "We're going to miss your father. He came in here all the time to do research, and he was so generous to the library." She gestured toward the computers. "It's thanks to him we have all these." She smiled before adding, "He said he couldn't see owning a computer himself, but he wanted to be sure that the folks in Bethel wouldn't be held back by not having access. Wasn't that good of him?"

Jonathan hadn't known any of this. It seemed consistent with his father's ways, though, parsimonious about spending for his personal convenience but lavish in spending to help others. It provoked in Jonathan a familiar anger. What arrogant humility.

He made some excuse to get away from the desk and wandered

through the low bookshelves, finding on them what he expected: new titles by best-selling authors and titles of local interest. There was a familiar smell to the place of musty carpet and
propane he associated with Bethel and nowhere else on earth.

He sat in a chair near the periodical section, where he picked
up one of the many farm periodicals and looked briskly through
the pages of ads for farm implements, herbicides, hybrid seed,
and pesticides. His father had once told him about how, after he
came back from his cfo duty in Virginia, he was the first farmer
in Seward County to embrace new farming methods. He'd been
hearing for months about this new thing — anhydrous ammo-
nia — the hottest trend for increasing yields, but he'd had to go
all the way to Omaha to get a tank since none of the local farm
co-ops were carrying it at that time. The other farmers around
him were skeptical about anhydrous, but his father said he hadn't
thought twice before applying it to his fields as recommended
and sitting back and watching it do wonders.

It wasn't until he was irrigating and he stooped down one day
to take a drink from the ditch — something he'd done all his
life — that he stopped himself, realizing the anhydrous would
have run off the field and into the ditch. That had set off a whole
chain of thought in his father. If he didn't feel comfortable drinking the water from those fields, why would he feel comfortable
selling the grain from them, even for animals to eat? He'd had
one field in sweet corn that year, and his father told Jonathan he
felt funny about putting that corn on his table. That had been it
for him — the first and last year his father ever used chemical on
his fields, even when everyone around him in the past half century had adopted it with enthusiasm. "By now," his father always
said, "they were all addicted to it, well in the clutches of agri-
business." He'd fought for years to amend the farm bill, arguing

that government subsidies should be for farmers, not crops. How pleased he'd been with the recent efforts of what he called "the young people" to make these issues a national concern.

The librarian interrupted Jonathan's thoughts to say, "There's a computer free, Mr. Grebel."

Before dressing for the viewing that evening, Elsa wanted to straighten the bedroom. It had gotten so overrun with the kids' things, she could hardly move. Once she'd finished, she locked the door and lay down on the bed in her slip, telling herself she'd finish dressing soon but right now she needed a little rest.

She had no idea how much time had passed when she woke from a dream that she'd locked herself in the chicken coop. In her dream the air in the chicken coop was dusty and foul as the hens flapped and squawked around her. She was holding a full bucket of eggs and kept rattling the door, frantic to get out.

"Gram Gram. You in there?" Timothy shook the doorknob. "Everyone's already left, Gram. I'm waiting to drive you into town."

"I must have fallen asleep. I'll be right there, Timothy."

Groggy and disoriented, Elsa rose from the bed. She'd never liked sleeping in the middle of the day.

When she and Zeke had been kids, Marian had always insisted they take naps after school. Their rooms had been next to one another, and every day Zeke would knock on her wall and sneak into her room, where they played together quietly, letting Marian think they were asleep.

Zeke had all sorts of ideas. He liked to crawl out his bedroom window at night with a flashlight and wander around the farm. They'd been little kids when they'd first done that together. Sometimes — a lot of times — his ideas tended toward the malicious, especially when it came to Marian. He'd once tried to convince Elsa to bake cookies and to substitute rabbit droppings for chocolate chips. Zeke had been delighted with the idea and had wheedled and wheedled her to help, but Elsa had refused, one of the rare times she'd stood up to him. He'd shocked Elsa one day when he told her he hated Marian so much he wanted to kill her.

As they got older, Zeke continued to sneak out at night without her. Elsa had known he was meeting friends and drinking alcohol, meeting up with girls from Seward and doing all sorts of things. Looking back, she probably shouldn't have been surprised when he enlisted.

She remembered then a time when she and Zeke were sitting on the bed on either side of their mother while she read to them. Elsa remembered Zeke saying something that caused Mama to throw back her head with laughter. Elsa saw again in memory Zeke's inquisitive little face. She remembered, too, the softness of Mama's arm as she leaned against her. Surely, this was one of her earliest memories, and she realized Mama must have already been sick with the bad heart that would finally take her life. She and Zeke had been in Mama's sickbed and not known it.

She took from the closet the dark-brown dress she wore for serious occasions. She'd made it when she was in her thirties, and she was proud of having taken good care of it so it had lasted all these years. She was proud, too, of being able to wear things she'd worn as a young woman. Haven always told her she was still beautiful to him. When she was a young woman, she couldn't have imagined how much life there was still in a person as she grew old.

Some days Anna June didn't want to go home. Before she even got to the driveway, she could see the haze — that was what she called it — something around the house that made it look like a fuzzy picture. On days like that she went straight to Grandma and Grandpa's house instead and asked Grandma to radio her mom and say she was staying at their place.

She only liked it at home when her dad was "in the dumps." That's what her mom called it. Then he just slept all day and sometimes talked to Anna June but didn't come to the kitchen to eat with them or talk to them too much. It was when he got all wound up that Anna June wanted to stay away. He had all kinds of ideas when he got like that, and he wanted them all to listen to him. At those times Anna June felt like he was crushing her brain. Her older sisters, Susan and Laurie, said, "He's all up in your business." When Anna June couldn't stay away — and she knew she was sinful for thinking it — she hated her dad. He scared her. If her mom wasn't as excited as he was, he said she was an idiot. Her mom cried a lot, but secretly, because if you ever cried in front of him when he was happy, watch out. He got furious with you. He forgot about all the days and days and days when he had cried. When he was excited, he couldn't remember anything from before. That was a secret, though. Even Celia couldn't know it. Whenever Celia came over, Anna June felt sad for her dad because people looked at him funny.

Today wasn't one of those days. Today she just didn't want to go home because she didn't want to get ready for the viewing. Her mom had found her at Grandma's house and told her to head home and take a bath and get dressed, but Anna June didn't want to see Grandpa dead. She'd seen her other grandpa when he was dead, and it was terrible. She'd been worrying about it all day.

The dress she had to wear that night was scratchy. She hated it. While Mom was combing her hair, Daddy was crying and saying he wasn't going to go.

"I don't want to go either," Anna June said, and Mom got mad. She said, "I don't need two children."

After Mom left the room, Anna June went to sit beside Daddy. She felt sorry now that she knew about Daniel. She laid her head on his shoulder and patted him on the back.

"It's all right, Daddy," she said. He cried harder when she said that. "It's all right. Daniel's all right. I saw him."

She felt Daddy get stiff beside her. He stopped crying and pushed Anna June away. "What the——" he said. "What the——" he said again, and this time he pushed her away farther. "What'd you say?"

"I don't know," Anna June said. "I'm sorry, Daddy."

He narrowed his eyes at her. "Where'd you hear that name?"

She felt afraid of him. "I don't know."

"Quit your lying to me."

"Daddy," she said and started to cry. "It's okay. Just pretend I didn't say it."

Mom interrupted them. She stood in the doorway. "In the car. Now. Both of you. No arguments tonight. I mean it." She could get like that.

Anna June was glad for the interruption. Even the scratchy

dress was okay. She hoped Daddy would forget she had said anything. He was sulking in the front seat of the car while Mom
was driving, and Mom patted his arm. She thought Daddy was
feeling bad about Grandpa, but Anna June knew it wasn't that.

Sure enough, Daddy turned to look at her in the backseat.
"You little busybody," he said. "You little shit busybody."

"Jeffrey!" Mom said.

"Stay out of this, woman."

Mom got quiet. Daddy said, "I shouldn't be surprised all this
old crap would surface now. That's how things work around
here." He looked back at her. "Missy, you don't know what kind
of a can of worms you've opened."

"Daddy," Anna June said and started to cry. Mom looked at
Daddy in her nervous way. She didn't like it when they were out
in public and he got nasty like he could. She slowed down the
car like she might turn around and go back home.

"Oh, no you don't," Daddy said. "We're going to the viewing
tonight. We're the bereaved. We're the fucking bereaved, and by
god, we're going to put on a show for the town."

"Jeffrey. Please don't."

"Yep. You heard me. We're the fucking bereaved. This is
the bereaved family of the deceased." Anna June hoped Mom
would stay quiet since when Daddy got like this it was better
not to fight him. Anna June tried to make herself small as she
sat back against the car seat and looked out the window at the
fields passing by. The corn here was still tall and straight. It was
hard to think that only a little ways away the fields had been ru-
ined by the storm the night before. It was unfair. Why would
God do that? Anna June wanted to cry for Mr. Slocum and for
the other farmers who'd lost their crops.

In the front seat Daddy was talking to himself, but she wasn't
listening. She was pretending she was someone else.

Timothy wasn't used to the Honda Civic's manual transmission, and the car bucked and died a couple times before he finally got it out of the driveway. Elsa hadn't been off the farm for three days, but it felt like a lifetime since she'd last seen the familiar landmarks on this road. She was always surprised those times when her own life was coming apart at how the world kept going on. Anytime she'd suffered a major loss, this same jarring contrast, everyone going about their business as though nothing had changed. She twisted a white hanky in her hands as Timothy drove. How she dreaded talking to all those people at the funeral home tonight.

"You gonna be all right, Gram Gram?"

"Right as I can be, Timothy."

"We have a little time. Did you want to see some of the damage in Seward County?"

At her nod Timothy stayed on past the turnoff for Bethel. Within only a few miles they saw the first signs of the storm's path—water still standing in fields and in ditches—but it wasn't until they were almost to Seward that they saw the full extent of the damage. Entire fields of corn were flattened, the tall stalks broken at the base. It looked like a giant foot had stepped across the country, destroying everything in its wake. "Timothy," was all she could say. Beside her Timothy nodded silently. As sorry as she felt, though, at seeing all this damage, she felt relieved too. Here were other people suffering, which was so much preferable to the indifference of everyone else.

Timothy pointed out an irrigation pivot that had been up-ended in a field looking now like a giant piece of twisted tinfoil. What was there to say? So much work for nothing. What could anyone say to that?

Already by six thirty Main Street was crowded with cars, forcing Jonathan down a gravel side street in search of a parking place. "Are all these cars in town because of your father?" Nina asked.

"I'm guessing so."

He parked finally in front of a block of modest, one-story houses typical of Bethel. All were well maintained, their cement stoops free of clutter, their walks swept clean. In front of each was a small lawn and flowers growing along the foundation.

As Jonathan parked, an elderly Mennonite couple came out of one of the houses. Jonathan recognized them. They weren't members of the Bethel church but attended instead one of the congregations that had splintered from the mother church years before. The man was tall and still powerfully built, and the woman was spare, almost birdlike. Nina noticed at the same time he did the resemblance to his parents. She gasped softly and laid her hand on his forearm.

"Are they related to you?" she said.

"No, but they're sure my folks' doppelgänger."

Inside Polsan's was abuzz with people and felt much more welcoming than it had the day before. He smelled coffee somewhere. Lord knows, you couldn't have a gathering of Mennonites without coffee. People stood in groups, some laughing, some somber. Among the crowd Jonathan saw his friends. He was glad they'd come to the farm the night before, so tonight their greetings felt casual and familiar.

Nina stayed beside him as they made their way to the coffin. Not surprisingly, his father didn't look at all like himself. His usually ruddy face looked ashen and overly made up, his cheeks sunken. His usually mobile and expressive mouth was now rigid; his thick white hair had been parted on the wrong side and combed too tight against his head. But it was his hands that most struck Jonathan; those large, work-weathered hands that had always been so alive, now looked like plaster casts. They were a yeasty yellow color, waxy and stiff. Jonathan stepped back slightly. He'd seen all he needed to see.

Once they'd turned away, Jonathan saw his aunts across the room and headed toward them. Tonight his father's death had become real to everyone again, and while his aunts had been merry for the last two days, all three of them were now sober and tearful. They each hugged Jonathan, and he felt enveloped not only by their ample flesh but by their ample generosity as well.

There was a stir in the room then, and Jonathan saw his mother and Tim had arrived. He'd turned back again to his aunts when he sensed a new commotion, some sort of agitation by the casket followed by a murmuring through the crowd that eventually became clear to him. "Jonathan. Where's Jonathan? She's asking for Jonathan." His heart quickened at her summons. His mother was asking for him. She needed him. He responded with urgency, weaving through the room, impatient as his progress was slowed by the crowd around him. I'm coming, he thought. I'm coming, Mother.

After he'd finally made it to her side, he bent toward her — tiny woman, fragile, vulnerable — he bent to give her his complete support, offering himself to her, whatever her need. "I'm here, Mother," he said and reached for her.

When they finally pulled up in front of Polsan's, there were cars lining the street. She felt a little thrill of pride that so many people had come out to honor Haven. She took a deep breath, and together she and Timothy entered the room. She was grateful Timothy was there as he held her arm. A path was made for them. She was hugged and caressed all the while being conveyed to the casket standing against the far wall. When she reached it, she couldn't even see clearly for the shock.

It was surely the most expensive casket you could buy. She gasped, and Timothy, still at her side, put a reassuring arm across her shoulder. Surely everyone had already noticed and formed as low an opinion of her and Haven as they possibly could over the opulence of that casket. It was an abomination, a mockery of everything she and Haven had stood for all their lives, pure vanity and ostentation. This was surely Jonathan's doing, his revenge against her after all this time, his final insult to her and his father.

Elsa gasped again, and this time people who were nearby rushed to her side. They tried to soothe her, misunderstanding her emotion for grief.

"Where's Jonathan?" she said. "I want to see him now."

She heard murmurs through the crowd as everyone searched for Jonathan, and within minutes he was at her side looking solicitous, seeming innocent of this outrage. When he attempted to touch her, she jerked her arm away from him. "How could you?" she whispered. "How could you?" She gestured toward the casket so he couldn't mistake her meaning.

"Don't worry about it, Mother. I paid for everything."

"Do you really think that's the only thing that concerns me?"

"Let's talk about this later, shall we, Mother."

"There won't be any later," she whispered. She couldn't help herself then. She wept with anger. She wasn't even sure she could say what the church brethren would think. It would be almost impossible for them to fathom such hypocrisy.

When he reached for her again, Elsa pulled away. "I asked you to do one thing for me. One thing, Jonathan, and you couldn't even do that."

"Mother, honestly, I only meant the best."

She looked at him. Did he really believe his own justification? Was his self-deception this great?

Then Jeffrey was there beside her. "Did you know about this?" she said.

"I tried to stop him, Mother, but I couldn't."

"Hogwash," Jonathan said, stepping forward.

Elsa could see he was eager to start a fight with his brother, and she took Jeffrey's arm, letting him steer her away. While she couldn't understand why Jeffrey hadn't been able to stop his brother, she knew how insistent Jonathan could be, especially when it came to things. He was craven about things. She didn't know where he had gotten to be such a materialist, but it was clear to her it was now his religion.

"I need to sit down," she said, and Jeffrey guided her to a chair against the wall, somehow fending off well-wishers at the same time. She could imagine how it must have gone, Jonathan arguing for the most expensive coffin. He had the means to pay for it, and that was the only criteria necessary for him. He'd abandoned all other values for the most base and vulgar displays of wealth. Whatever hope she may have kept in some small part of her heart that he was still a good man she now dismissed. He was truly lost to them, beyond prayer and among the damned.

"I want to talk to someone at Polsan's," she finally said to Jeffrey.

No one paid any mind to Anna June where she sat on a chair against the wall at the funeral home. The good thing about her dad acting up was that her mom ignored her and stayed close to Daddy in case he got upset. Anna June listened too, just in case they'd need to leave early.

Instead, it was Grandma who acted up. Anna June heard her across the room. "No," she said. "No, no, no, no." Everyone got nervous when that happened. "She's taking it awful hard," Anna June heard someone say, but Anna June knew it wasn't that. Grandma wasn't sad; she was mad. But who was she mad at? Was she mad at Grandpa for dying? Was she still mad at Anna June? Anna June kept listening, but she couldn't sort it out. It felt like a bright light was flashing everywhere and making it hard to see. She felt sick to her stomach from it.

That's when Nina found her. She sat down beside Anna June.

"I wonder what's going on. Do you have any idea what's happening?" she said. Anna June shook her head no, and Nina went on. "I wish someone in this family would tell me what's going on. I feel like such an outsider sometimes."

Anna June looked at Nina quickly to see if she was serious.

She seemed not to understand she was an outsider. She would always be an outsider. Finally, when Anna June didn't say anything, Nina took the hint and left.

Celia's family came just in the nick of time. "Is that your Grandma?" Celia asked after she sat down beside Anna June.

"Yes."

"What's wrong with her?"

"Beats me. She's upset about something."

"Is it about your grandpa?"

"I don't think so."

Celia nodded her head. She hugged Anna June. "Let's go to the car," she said, and Anna June was glad to follow her outside. Fritz was there in the backseat. When he saw Anna June and Celia, he went crazy jumping on the window and barking. They got inside, and he jumped on Anna June and licked her face. He wiggled all over, he was so happy to see her. Once Fritz settled down on her lap, he licked her hand slowly, and she petted his long soft ears. It made her feel happy to have him there on her lap.

"Is it bad?" Celia said.

"Pretty bad."

"Let's go swimming every day next week."

"Okay," Anna June said. She thought about seeing all the kids from school again, and she wasn't sure she wanted to do it.

"I saw Natalie Dirstein at the pool two days ago," Celia said. "She got her hair cut really short. It looks amazing." Celia pulled her hair back tight and showed it to Anna June. "Would I look okay with my hair short?" She looked at herself in the rearview mirror and moved her head around a little before she looked back at Anna June again.

"It looks okay to me," Anna June said. She didn't care about things like that. Her mom wore a prayer veil, but her older sisters didn't, and Anna June had already cut her hair short a long time ago. Celia still wore her hair long like her mom's but hadn't started to wear it up the way the Mennonite women in Bethel did even if they didn't wear the veil.

"Mom says I can cut my hair," Celia said. She was still holding her hair back and looked at herself again before letting it down. "I think I'll do it. Do you think I should?"

Celia's mom and dad got into the car before Anna June could answer. Fritz jumped over the seat and onto her mom's lap. "Celia, call Fritz, will you?" her mom said. "He's going to snag my hose." She turned to look at Anna June. "Oh, you poor little thing," her mom said. "I wish we could just take you home with us."

"Could she come home with us?" Celia said.

"That'd be fine with me," her mom said, "but I'm guessing her family wants her to stay with them."

Celia's dad looked at her. "Come stay with Celia all next week if you want, okay kiddo?"

Anna June nodded. She wanted to cry a little because they were being so nice to her. "I'd better go back inside," Anna June said to be polite so they could go home.

She got out of the car and watched as they pulled away. Every time she looked at the funeral home, she smelled a strong smell, like the smell of skunks. It was still light outside, and she decided to sit on a bench on the sidewalk out front. People came and went and said hello to her.

Across the street was the hardware store where Grandpa took her when he did errands, and farther down the street was the lumberyard where they went when he needed to build a fence or fix something on one of the outbuildings. She knew all the shop owners. Mr. Hostetler always gave her a piece of gum when she went into the hardware store with Grandpa. "You got your helper with you," he'd say. The store was closed now, but she crossed the street and looked in. There were dusty antique tools in the window. Farther back in the store, she could see the rows of things. She knew where the nails and screws and bolts and hinges were. If she'd been old enough to drive the truck into town, Grandpa had said he would have sent her alone to get what he needed from Mr. Hostetler. She could have done it fine. He'd told her so.

Mr. Hostetler came around the corner while she was looking in the window. He was wearing a suit and tie. She'd never seen him dressed up before, so she knew he'd been over to the funeral home.

"Good evening, Miss Anna June," he said. He shook his head when he said that. "You were sure your grandpa's girl." He shook his head again. "I didn't know a better man than your grandpa, and that's the solemn truth." Anna June nodded. "You come see me anytime, you hear."

Anna June liked Mr. Hostetler saying that, but she sort of wished he'd quit saying nice things. She didn't want to cry in front of him.

"I better get," she said.

"Like I said, you come in and see me anytime."

When she got back to the viewing, everybody kept saying she should go look at Grandpa. "He looks good," they said, which just went to show how stupid they were. Whenever Anna June looked toward the coffin, she saw worms everywhere. It was terrible. She'd decided she wasn't going to look at Grandpa no matter what. Her mom had told her she should look at him so she'd believe it was real, like she didn't already believe it was real. That was plain stupid, and Anna June ignored all of them.

After the crowd had thinned later that evening, Jeffrey found Jonathan and elbowed him hard in the ribs, an old trick from his days playing basketball. "Sorry," he said, and anyone listening, except Jonathan, would have thought it was a sincere apology. When later he brought his heel down hard on Jonathan's foot with yet another half-assed apology, Jonathan retaliated with a shove. People noticed, of course, but what they saw was Jonathan's aggression, not Jeffrey's provocation. Jonathan waited until attention had been diverted away from them again before he whispered, "That's low even for you, Jeff. You know very well you encouraged me to buy that casket."

"I didn't encourage you to do anything, Jon. I only said aloud what you were thinking, that it was a fine piece of craftsmanship and that Dad would have admired it." Jonathan thought back to the day before. While this was technically true, Jeffrey had never spoken out against the purchase. He'd watched in silence as Jonathan laid down his credit card. He'd said encouraging things the entire time. As they'd driven home afterward, he'd given no hint it had been a bad idea. But hadn't Jonathan himself suspected it was a bad idea? Why had he looked to Jeffrey

for feedback, trusted him like he had? Why had he been so sus-
ceptible to the opinion of that smarmy mortician, Brad Benson?
Jonathan couldn't understand his own stupidity. After all these
years he was still Jeffrey's instrument to punish their mother,
still Jeffrey's willing dupe.

"So you feeling pretty good right now, Jon?" Jeffrey said. "You
feeling pretty superior about things?" Jonathan thought he was
still talking about the casket, until Jeffrey said, "You feeling pretty smart, telling Anna June about Daniel?" Jeffrey had lowered
his voice when he said Daniel's name, but still Jonathan felt a
nervous shock at hearing it spoken aloud. They both paused a
second at the transgression. It felt radical for them even now as
grown men to say the forbidden name of their brother.

"I didn't tell Anna June anything," Jonathan said.

"I know it was you who told her."

"There you are truly mistaken, Jeff. She already knew about
it. I took her to the pond last night to see where the accident happened, and she asked about him. What could I do? I told her
what happened."

"It wasn't your place to fill in the details."

"Don't you think it's about time we grew up, Jeff?"

Jeffrey ignored him. "After this, Jon, there's really no reason
for you ever to come back here again."

"After what?"

"After we've laid our father to rest, you moron."

"So, you're telling me I've done more harm to this family than
anyone else? You're telling me that, you freeloading son of a bitch?"

Jeffrey laughed as though he were above it all. He'd always
been above it all, entitled to whatever it was he wanted.

"You owe Mother an explanation about the casket at least,
Jeff. You know very well I didn't buy it out of spite."

"You're so full of shit, Jon."

"You know, Jeff, I've always wondered how it is you can stand yourself."

"And I've wondered the same thing about you."

As Jonathan watched Jeffrey shuffle away, a large man gone to seed, he remembered something he'd forgotten, a long-ago scene between Jeffrey and his mother. It must have been shortly after Daniel had died. His mother had gotten out the bowl they used for ritual foot washings and was attempting to wash Jeffrey's feet. Jeffrey had been a handsome young man, and in those days he carried himself with the confidence of an athlete. But Jonathan remembered now how on that occasion Jeffrey shrank away from their mother. He seemed literally to shrink as he shook his head no and backed away from her.

Jonathan couldn't remember a single word being spoken between them, nor could he recall his father being present, but understanding as he did the meaning of the Mennonite foot washing as an act of humility — requiring the one washing to act as a servant and the one receiving to humble himself in order to allow for the intimate invasion of privacy — Jonathan guessed his mother was admitting to wrongdoing, asking, through this abjection, Jeffrey's forgiveness. How could Jeffrey, though, have seen it any way other than as an act of aggression? That same arrogant humility again, the competitive martyrdom that was in its own way as violent as anything Jonathan had ever encountered. Of course Jeffrey couldn't accept her request for forgiveness. What did it say that she had asked for it except to suggest it was Jeffrey who needed forgiveness? And by refusing her, Jeffrey would be kept in thrall to her, as she would be to him. Eventually, Daniel was erased from the powerful bond between Jeffrey and their mother. All that remained was their silence, their guilt, their terrible hatred of one another.

Elsa found Brad Benson that evening before she left. He was standing against the wall near the guest book. "Could we talk?" she said, and he silently motioned for her to follow him into a back room.

"What can I do for you, Mrs. Grebel?"

"There's been a terrible mistake."

She saw his face grow a little pale at this, and she went on. "My son. My son Jonathan bought a very expensive coffin for his father." She raised her eyebrows, hoping he'd get what she was saying. He didn't help her in any way. "It isn't our way. You understand. I need to make a change before the funeral."

"Mrs. Grebel." Brad Benson cleared his throat. "This presents something of a problem. I'm sure you'll understand. We can't return a unit that's been used, you see."

"How used has it been? Who would know?"

"Mrs. Grebel."

Elsa sat up straighter. "I'm not satisfied with the product, Mr. Benson. It's that simple."

She watched Brad Benson's face carefully. She saw a sliver of impatience behind his eyes, but his voice never wavered. "Our policy is clear, Mrs. Grebel, and your sons signed off on that. There are no returns."

At this Elsa straightened again. She didn't like this young man, this Brad Benson. Who did he think he was — this man young enough to be her grandson talking to her like she was a child? She felt sure Haven could have reasoned with him. She'd known the original owners, the Polsan family. They'd sold the mortuary only a couple years before. She didn't know who the new owners were. "I'd like to speak to the owner," she said.

Brad Benson paused for a second. "You're talking to him," and Elsa thought she heard a tinge of pride in his voice.

Elsa felt her shoulders sag. She finally stood up. "You can be sure I'll remember this," she said and walked away with as much dignity as she could manage.

This time when she returned to the casket, she allowed herself to look at Haven. She touched one of his hands. She smoothed his hair and tried to part it the right way, finally giving up as the hairspray they'd used held it fast. She was glad to have this time alone with him. The room was almost empty, and she didn't see her two sons anywhere. Anna June was across the room sitting in a chair looking miserable. Elsa wondered if she'd even looked at her grandfather. She tried to catch Anna June's eye to wave her over, but Anna June didn't look at her.

It was Nina who finally came to stand beside her. She rested her arm across Elsa's shoulder, and Elsa leaned into her a little. She guessed Nina hadn't known anything about Jonathan buying the casket.

"He was one of the most remarkable men I ever met," Nina said. "I always told all my friends in Boston about Jonathan's father, this amazing organic farmer who lived in Nebraska, this man who traveled the world on peace missions." Elsa didn't respond. She didn't need anyone to tell her about the worth of her husband. "You about ready to go home?" Nina said after a few minutes.

"Yes. I came with Timothy."

"I'll go find him," Nina said.

Elsa took a deep breath. She looked at Haven one last time. She felt a chill run deep through her soul. She cast about for a Scripture and came up empty except for one: "There are many mansions in my father's house. I go there now to prepare a place for you." She knew it wasn't the right interpretation of that Scripture, but she felt comforted by the idea that Haven had gone on before her, that he'd be waiting there for her when her time came.

Pastor Roth had been at the viewing earlier, but she didn't see him now. She supposed she'd talked to Brad Benson longer than she'd realized. She supposed, too, the scene over the casket had been disturbing for those who had noticed it. Word would spread quickly. She wanted to ask Pastor Roth what he believed about heaven. The Scriptures said there would be no marriage in heaven, and it had made her sad all day thinking about that. She wondered if maybe Pastor Roth couldn't shed some light on her questions.

Daddy was still in a mood when they drove back home. He laughed about Jonathan. He called him a fool. "He thinks he's such hot shit," he said. Both Anna June and Mom stayed quiet. They hoped he'd sleep it off by the next morning. Anna June was glad he hadn't done anything too embarrassing at the viewing.

She rested her head against the window and looked into the night sky. The stars were out. Otherwise, it felt very dark. There were farm lights along the road, and something about those lights made her feel lonely. There was a lonely feeling about the world. She thought about how no one really knew anyone else, not even her own family. Anna June had things inside her no one knew about, things she would never tell anyone, and tonight she saw how everyone had those places in them. She felt like she wasn't a little girl anymore. If Grandpa had been alive, she might have asked him about what she was feeling. He'd have listened anyway. But now there was no one to talk to like that.

She wanted to break her promise to Timothy about sleeping with Grandma. He'd been wrong about things. Grandma didn't need them to stay with her. But Anna June didn't want to stay at home with Daddy the way he was.

"Mom," she said. "Drop me off at Grandma's house."

It was long past dark by the time he and Nina got back to the house. "I'm going to walk a little," Jonathan said as they got out of the car. Nina looked around at the dark prairie but didn't say anything, instead kissing him good night. He hadn't told her what had happened with his mother earlier, but he could tell by her respectful silence she knew something was up.

"You want me to take your jacket inside with me?"

"Thanks." Jonathan handed it to her. He watched as she walked to the house before turning to go into the pasture. In the distance he heard the laughing yelp of a coyote celebrating a kill. Soon it was joined by the howls of the pack. Jonathan thought there was no sound in the world as soul piercingly lonely as that of the coyote.

He was distracted by these thoughts, a welcome distraction from thinking about his mother, when he felt a familiar jolt of energy, a feeling he'd experienced throughout his boyhood whenever he'd crossed this same place in the pasture, a spot near where their fence met the neighboring farm's fence, in a little gully filled with wild plum and sumac. No matter how distracted he'd been as a boy while playing in this pasture, he'd felt this same pulse near that fence. He'd always believed it must have been an Indian burial ground or the site of a battle or a massacre. Though he'd never discovered any historical evidence to corroborate his theory, there was definitely some sort of rupture, some sort of psychic energy, in this spot.

He sat down right there in the pasture, not worrying about how the damp grass would ruin his good linen pants. While traveling one time in Australia, he and Monty had hooked up for a while with an Aboriginal man. This thoroughly modern man was a linguist working for the Australian government. They'd been driving together through a long stretch of desolate country when suddenly the guy insisted they stop. Jonathan and Monty had watched from the car as he got out and performed some sort of ritual that involved singing and chanting.

Once he'd gotten back into the car, he told them about Dreamtime and the need to honor the god in whose region you were conceived. This was where he'd been conceived, he told them, and went on to explain how the world had to be remade each day, that it had to be sung into being, and if you ignored your duty, the world would cease to exist. Jonathan remembered how he and Monty had laughed, thinking the guy was teasing them, trying to get one over on the visitors, but the guy hadn't thought it was funny at all. He still believed he had to perform those rituals. It had surprised Jonathan, an enlightened man still practicing those ancient beliefs that way.

He half-jokingly wondered tonight if maybe he'd been conceived in this spot. A ridiculous notion, of course, knowing his parents as he did, but he remembered how the Aboriginal man had told Jonathan and Monty he felt the gods' energy like a magnetic pull. Was that what Jonathan always felt here, a kind of magnetic energy. Such metaphysical feelings had to be the source of all religious inspiration, didn't they? The various attempts to explain the unexplainable.

Monty, of all his friends, could entertain conversations of this nature. He'd grown up in Montana in a strict Baptist home. And like Jonathan, he'd left home at eighteen and never looked back. They'd bonded over the commonalities in their past and enjoyed highly speculative, at times verging toward silly, theories about the meaning of life.

Overall Jonathan didn't know if he really believed friendship was anything more than mutual self-interest. Most friends, as he saw it anyway, were really potential enemies, since only someone you knew intimately could be harmful enough to be an enemy. Maybe because of that, he'd always considered Monty more like a brother. Certainly he'd been more of a brother to Jonathan than Jeffrey had ever been.

They'd met in Australia, both of them in Adelaide when they witnessed a ridiculous accident in which the driver of a vehicle had decided to use the sidewalk to get around traffic and in his haste had run over a postal box. Monty, at that time a stranger on the street, shook his head and said, "That guy's up fuck creek with a paddle up his ass," and Jonathan, recognizing him as a fellow American, had asked where he was from. "A little no-account, shithole ranch in northern Montana, near the Blackfeet reservation." They'd gone together for a drink afterward and from that chance meeting had traveled together for over a year, leaving Australia for Africa and parts of Asia, finally ending their travels in Goa.

It was late, and later still in Boston, but Jonathan decided to see if out here he couldn't get a signal on his cell phone. He took it as a good sign when he heard the phone ringing on the other end of the line.

When Monty finally picked up, he sounded groggy. "That you, Jonathan?" he said.

"Sure is, buddy. I'm sorry to call so late."

"What's up?"

"I'm just out here in the middle of a pasture on my dad's place, my ass wet from sitting in the grass, and I started thinking about the meaning of life."

Monty laughed.

"I need you to talk to me tonight, buddy," Jonathan said.

"How's everything going?"

"About like you'd expect."

"That bad?"

"Talk to me, man," Jonathan said again, and without questioning him, Monty talked. He was half-asleep as he described in detail his search for a new coffee grinder, recounted what was happening in the office and what was happening in the city. Jonathan felt soothed by the banality of his report.

"You feeling more like yourself now?" Monty finally said.

"Sure am."

"Just remember, you're stronger than dirt."

Jonathan laughed uneasily. "Thanks for reminding me of that, buddy. I'll see you in a couple days."

He was still smiling when he hung up the phone. Stronger than dirt, one of their shorthand references to Jonathan's past. He'd sometimes wished Monty could let things go, especially when it came to Lisa, but it wasn't his way. He had to remind Jonathan with these little jabs how closely entwined their lives were. This particular saying was in reference to Jonathan's darkest moment.

His own rock bottom hadn't been losing Karalee but, rather, his headlong free fall after they'd split and the sordid attachment — the obsession really — he'd formed with Lisa, a woman so foul, so narcissistic, that he'd finally found the punishment he'd been looking for. The woman stank, for god's sake. She lived in absolute squalor. And beneath all that degradation there was no heart of gold. No, in fact she'd thought she was too good for Jonathan. She'd laughed at his background, sneered at his rural education, mocked his loss of Karalee, and belittled the dilemma with Tim and his parents. She considered him weak, "a gutless wimp."

"Isn't that sort of redundant?"

"Even your sense of humor is idiotic," she'd said.

Finally, though, her goading got to him, made him want to prove himself. He'd begged her to marry him after a long weekend when they'd both been strung out, so messed up he'd wondered if he'd ever find his way out of it, but she'd scorned his proposal. That was when he'd finally decided to get his college degree, to prove he was worthy of her. By the time he applied to graduate school, he'd thankfully left her far in the past.

He'd learned something about the injustice of the world from that situation. Lisa hadn't been some lowlife down on her luck. They'd met in Goa and later moved to Paris. She was the daughter of a diplomat, a privileged girl getting back at daddy. Sorbonne educated, she spoke five languages. Her little heroin habit was only a slight detour. Her father eventually paid for expensive rehab, set her up in an apartment. She stepped back with ease into the life she'd been destined to live, married a French banker, and, as far as Jonathan knew, was still a respectable society matron living in Paris. Before they split, she'd accused him one last time of being weak, to which he'd oddly responded that in fact he was stronger than dirt. Monty had laughed the first time Jonathan had told him about this silly comeback, and he'd never let him forget it.

It had been that whole situation, though, that had redefined for Jonathan the tenor of his relationship with Monty. When it was finally over, Monty had said, "I thought you were probably making a mistake taking up with her, but I just figured we'd get through whatever happened." It had been a revelation to Jonathan, that sort of acceptance.

He lay back and took in the expanse above him. The sky was thick with stars stretching from horizon to horizon. One small cloud moved slowly across the moon and was outlined for a few minutes by its silver light. Funny how he never thought about the sky at all when he was in Boston, but when he was here in Nebraska, it was everywhere. You couldn't not notice the sky and the way it made you feel at once infinitesimal and at the center of everything. Tonight Jonathan quieted his mind and emptied himself into that vast space, felt blotted out by the immediacy of the indifferent earth.

The seat of his pants was damp as he walked back to the house later. He felt exhausted by the day and its interactions but oddly calmed by the land.

Her sisters had been subdued after the viewing. Two late nights in a row and an early start the next morning for the funeral had sent them all to bed as soon as they'd gotten home. Timothy had also gone up to bed. Elsa couldn't quite face her room, knowing Anna June and Timothy would be there again tonight. She didn't understand why she couldn't tell them to sleep somewhere else.

She sat alone at the kitchen table for a long time, listening to the ticking of the rooster clock. The kitchen was dark except for the stove light. There were rustlings here and there as people prepared for bed, but no one disturbed her solitude. Tomorrow after the funeral almost everyone would be leaving.

She had thought she was the last one up when Jonathan surprised her at the kitchen door. He was still wearing his suit pants, and they were rumpled and damp. Even in the dim light, she could see the way his jaw set tight when he saw her.

Neither of them spoke for a few minutes. "I'd like to sit with you for a while, Mother," Jonathan finally said. When she didn't respond, he pulled out a kitchen chair. "Could I get you anything?"

"No, Jonathan. I don't want anything from you."

He turned his head away, seeming to her suddenly like the little boy she'd known and loved. They sat together in silence for a long time, listening as the old house creaked and groaned around them.

"I would have liked to nurse him awhile," Elsa finally said, surprising herself with the remark. "I'd have liked to have had a little time to say good-bye," she added.

"Who are you talking about?"

Elsa looked up at Jonathan, surprised by his obtuseness. "Your father. Who else?"

Jonathan looked at her closely, and she began to feel uncomfortable under his gaze. "What about Daniel, Mother?" he finally said. "What about Daniel?"

Hearing that name again even after all these years cut her heart in half. Elsa shook her head; she felt a searing pain and clutched her chest.

"Mother, I'm not trying to hurt you," Jonathan said. "But can't you see how it's always here. It's always been here standing between all of us, making all of us into liars."

"What do you want from me?"

"Nothing, Mother. I don't want anything from you."

She looked at Jonathan. He was no longer a young man. He'd lived an entire life incomprehensible to her. She couldn't imagine what he was after, bringing up the past like this, but most certainly he wanted something.

"All I want is for us to start being honest as a family," Jonathan went on, making no sense to her. Him — the least honest among them — asking her to be honest? She'd sacrificed for years to raise his son for him. She'd picked up the pieces after the mess he'd made of his life with that Karalee woman, and in return his thanks to her was this insistence on bringing up the painful past?

"I think we've said entirely enough tonight, Jonathan."

"We haven't said anything, Mother. What about Daniel? What about what happened after Daniel?"

Elsa winced as he said the name again. "The Lord calls us to go forward, not to get mired in what can't be changed," she said.

"He calls us to be honest about our lives, to take stock of ourselves, to reckon with our past mistakes. Aren't we called to exhort one another daily?" Jonathan said.

"The Devil knows how to quote Scripture too, Jonathan."

"It isn't only me, Mother. The aunts see it too. Everyone who knows you sees it."

Elsa held up a hand to stop him. "That's enough. You won't enlist others to your ends."

"I'm sorry, Mother. I know you've suffered so much in your life. I don't want to cause you more hurt. Your life hasn't been easy . . ."

Elsa shook her head. "And you won't manipulate me into self-pity."

Jonathan sighed. "We can't seem to get past it, can we? There's no way to talk about Daniel, about how it's damaged our family."

Elsa felt herself go rigid. There seemed to be nothing she could do to stop the tears. "Why are you hounding me so?" she finally managed to say.

At this Jonathan's face fell. He gestured as though he might hug her but stopped himself. "Just ignore me, Mother," he said. "I'm not myself."

"Oh, that's where you're wrong, Jonathan." She was horrified when a large involuntary sob broke through her lips as she spoke.

"Mother. Please." Jonathan started to get out of his chair, but she raised a hand to stop him. She didn't want his comfort. "I'm so sorry," he went on. "It was wrong of me to buy that casket. I knew you wouldn't want it, but I got caught up in something.

I'll admit that to you, but — " he paused. "But I won't apologize about Daniel."

Elsa felt another stab to her heart. Was he trying to kill her? I'll never recover from this, she thought. All those years ago, that dark, cold winter, having to face each day and each day feeling like she wanted nothing so much as to lay down beside her baby under the frozen earth. That's all she'd wanted back then was to sleep. Pastor Roth had come to visit. He'd prayed with her and told her she had a responsibility to the living so that she'd finally gotten up out of her bed. It had taken everything she'd had to do it, but she'd done the right thing. She'd stood up from her bed, and she'd never looked back. They'd all gone forward. She couldn't have looked at Jeffrey again if she'd been always living in the past. He was her son, and it was her duty to do right by him.

Beside her she saw Jonathan had started to weep. She felt nothing for him.

He took a ragged breath. "Don't make me more a villain than I am."

"It isn't my place to judge you, Jonathan. It's the Lord you'll have to face one day. May He be merciful to you."

"You're so hard on everyone you love."

"But you're wrong about that," Elsa said. "I fought for years that you would be brought back into God's grace. I still pray every day for you to be right with Him. And this very morning our dear Anna June repented of her great sin of pride. I fought for that child's soul even in the midst of my own hour of suffering. I searched for the lost lamb, and tonight she's back among the saved."

"I'm glad, Mother," Jonathan said, his voice flat, a tone she didn't recognize.

"Don't be glad, Jonathan. Thank the Lord for restoring the lost sheep to His flock."

Jonathan abruptly stood up from the table. He paused before he left the kitchen. "Don't worry about the casket tomorrow, Mother. I talked to Brad Benson tonight after everyone left. There'll be another casket at the funeral tomorrow, one you'll approve of."

"How will—"

"Don't worry. I paid for it."

Elsa said nothing. Did he expect her to be grateful that he'd righted his own wrong? He'd opened a place in her heart tonight, a place that had been sealed off for many years. She felt almost numb from the pain. She'd have to work hard to get it all packed away again where it belonged before the funeral tomorrow.

By the time Jonathan got back to their room, he was clenching his fists and muttering to himself. Nina was already asleep, and he woke her. "We're leaving tonight. We'll stay in Omaha until our flight leaves."

"Jonathan?" Nina said, still half-asleep. "What are you talking about?"

"We're leaving. I can't stay here another night."

"But the funeral —"

"I don't care about that."

"Did something more happen with your mother?"

"You could say that."

"I'm sorry, sweetie. I'll do whatever you want," Nina said, "but why don't we just get through the night and go first thing tomorrow morning, okay? We can leave as early as you want."

Jonathan had been sitting on the edge of the bed, and he dropped his face into his hands. Nina rubbed his back. "Why don't we get a decent night's sleep anyway?" she said. He didn't respond. After several minutes she said, "You know, Jonathan, yours isn't the only family that behaves badly when it's grieving."

"I didn't say we were."

He knew he wouldn't sleep, but it wasn't fair to Nina to leave at this hour. He sat like this for several minutes. Behind him he could hear Nina was still awake and listening. He looked out the window into the darkness beyond. He heard a rustling in the trees, and a screech owl chortled. When he finally turned his attention back to Nina, he could hear she had slipped back into sleep. He played over and over again what had happened that evening. He didn't know why he'd expected more from Jeffrey or why he'd tried with his mother. What had he thought would happen? His rubbed his neck but couldn't relieve the tension there.

He was still sitting on the side of the bed thinking his dark thoughts when at 3:10 he heard the piano in the living room. He knew it was his mother. She'd wake the whole damn house. When he stood up to go tell her to quiet down, Nina laid a hand on his arm to stop him. "Let her be," she said.

"She'll wake everyone."

"Let her. Poor thing. It's the only way she knows to cope."

Jonathan did not respond. Poor thing, my ass, he thought. She only looked vulnerable. She had a steel rod for a backbone and a heart of pure stone. He couldn't tell Nina this. She wouldn't understand, and he didn't want her to know the truth about his family. He'd never told her about Daniel, and he never would. He could hear Nina was still awake, and he finally patted her hand. "I'm just going out to sit with her. I won't disturb her."

Jonathan saw his mother there at the piano, looking ghostly in her white nightgown, her long hair unpinned and falling down her back. She was still slender, her posture erect. As he watched her play, he could imagine her as a girl. Tonight she played with such absorption she didn't know he was there. He finally sat down in his father's old chair to listen. Hymn after hymn. And then:

Blessed assurance, Jesus is mine!
Oh what a foretaste of glory divine.
Heir of salvation, purchase of God,
born of His spirit, washed in His blood.

This is my story, this is my song,
praising . . .

Jonathan must have been humming along, for his mother suddenly lifted her hands from the keys and turned from the piano.
"Haven," she said, her voice so hopeful it broke his heart a little.
"No, Mother. It's Jonathan. Sing with me." When she turned
back to the piano, she didn't immediately start to play again but
instead left her hands in her lap for a few minutes as if deciding
whether or not to continue. At last she raised her hands back
to the keyboard and began to play. She knew all the old hymns
by heart. Jonathan sang alone for a while before finally her alto
joined his baritone. Their voices had always harmonized well,
and they still did. When he'd been a kid, they'd sung duets together in church. After he'd left the farm and married Karalee,
whenever he came home to visit, she'd asked him to sing with
her, and he'd always refused.

In a few hours, he thought, they would bury his father, and
he would be there with them. He would sit in the front row between his wife and his mother. He would stand with his family
before the congregation. He would bow his head to pray, lift his
voice to sing, listen to the Scriptures and the words of comfort,
and follow his father's body to the graveyard, where he would be
buried. His mother would never again speak of what had happened earlier that night. His mother, the great refuser, would
refuse even to acknowledge his breach of the family contract by
mentioning Daniel. He would come back again later this summer. He would help her sort out her finances. He would show

her the bank balances and the mutual funds. He would help her move into a more comfortable house, if that was what she wanted, and he and Nina would help Anna June finish her angels.

Jeffrey would never forgive him for telling Anna June the truth about Daniel, but he, too, would keep the pact with the past and never mention it again. Except there was this: Anna June knew the truth about their life together, and one day she would break their long silence and tell the story of the true secret history of the Haven Grebel family. And there was this too. No matter how much time and distance he'd put between himself and this farm, it was in his bones. It was who he was as much as anything else, and he'd separated himself from it at a high price.

Outside he heard the night sounds slowly become the sounds of early morning. Across the prairie there was a great unfolding of the world. Outside the open window beside him he felt the earth waking. He felt it stirring to his very core.

To order or obtain more information on these or other University of Nebraska Press titles, visit www.nebraskapress.unl.edu.